Copyright

A

The characters and events portrayed in this book are fictitious. Any
similarity to real persons, living or dead, is coincidental and not
intended by the author.

No part of this book may be reproduced, or stored in a retrieval
system, or transmitted in any form or by any means, electronic,
mechanical, photocopying, recording, or otherwise, without
express written permission of the publisher.

ISBN-13: 9798801948911
ISBN-10: 1477123456

Cover design by: Sara McCelland. photograph by Scott Butcher
Library of Congress Control Number: 2018675309
Printed in the United States of America

This is dedicated to my father, who passed away this year. Love you Dad forever and always.

CONTENTS

FOREWORD

I'd like to thank everyone who contributed to Plain Jane. To beta readers, Di, Sara, Louise. To proof reader, Samira Shehadah Druilhe and for technical support Tammy Ann Chambers.

Special thanks to my family, my husband and two boys and my mum who supports me in everything I do.

Thank you for your friendship, love, skill and time.

Warning: *This book contains, mild sexual content, offensive language, sexual references.*

PLAIN JANE

Beastly Pursuits

Book one

CHAPTER 1

BETH

The first time I spotted him in the flesh was when my good friend Karen asked me to do her a favour. She had been working freelance as a special effects makeup artist for the last six years and had a lucrative contract with a company called Eve Sharp Designs, a subsidiary of DarkMatter Studios, working as part of their movie department makeup team in London.

Now, normally Karen, the perpetual night owl, could successfully wing it as a lark whenever the need arose with amazing fakery. Aided by a bucket load of perfect cover concealer, 'forever more' fresh eye drops and a gallon of mouthwash to hide the booze, no one would know she'd got in an hour before work started at the ungodly hour of four in the morning.

However, no amount of smoke and mirrors was ever going to help her out this time. After a night full of more than her usual quota of hot shots, she had taken a tumble, negotiating a spiral metal staircase in 5-inch heels, and broken her arm.

So, at the fabulous hour of three in the morning, I received a call from my injured buddy at All Saints hospital begging me to take her place that morning in the studio, 'to do a little powdering and preening for some bloke who needs to look moody and mysterious,' (her words, not mine), for his role in a series called Ironclaw.

After a frantic conversation with Karen, which comprised me saying repeatedly like a Tourette's-inflicted Polly; no, no, no, she ended the conversation with the immortal words; "Don't worry, chick, it will be a doddle."

I'm not sure what happened, but in a wink a car pulled up outside the tiny studio apartment I shared with two friends, to transport me into the back lot of studio 12. Wiggling uncomfortably in my seat, I did a mental snapshot on how I'd dressed that morning -(or middle of the night according to my internal clock) - and grimaced.

"Jeez, luv, are you a makeup artist?" asked the driver as he opened the car door and handed me a sheet with Karen's makeup guide on it.

As I looked down at myself, I guessed he wasn't just being uncharitable. I could have sworn I'd put on my stylish pink sailor pants and a cream camisole, but apparently some elf had pulled a blinder on me and substituted them with orange clown pants and a puke-coloured top. In my dazed state, I'd also dug out a polka dot bra that no longer fitted. The night before, I'd gone to bed with an intensive hair repair mask on, which I had intended to rinse off the next morning. Because of this, I had stuffed on the first hat I had come across to hide the rat's tails and failed to look in the mirror. So, here I was, dressed like a tramp with greasy looking hair and a face, bare of any sort of enhancement, going to the most important gig of my life!

The chauffeur kept eying me in the rear-view mirror

and my hopes soared. Perhaps I didn't look as bad as I feared. After the fourth time, I ventured a smile and, encouraged by my friendliness, my admirer asked, "It's not catching, is it? Only I've got kids, and I really don't want them to come down with whatever you've got."

"What?" I said, dashing my fingers over my face.

"That red rash, none of my lot has had chicken pox."

"Chicken pox?" I said, trying to look at myself in the reflection of the door windows.

There was only one thing I was likely to be allergic to in a hair preparation, and Hannah promised me the hair treatment she'd persuaded me to try didn't have coconut in it. I took hold of a soggy strand and inhaled it as if I was a wine connoisseur. Liar! I thought with a groan.

"Oh, it only came on this morning. Could be anything," I said with an evil smile.

The man gulped. "Are you sure they want you in today? They won't want to spread that to the cast. They have enough problems with the gastric flu that's going around."

"Eve's insisted. They're desperate."

"They would have to be," he said, focusing his attention back on the road.

We pulled up at the studio as my heart drove into my chest. What am I doing here? Can I even do this?

Eve barged out of the building like an express train, her arms pumping like pistons as she ploughed her way to my door and yanked it open. Grabbing my arm, she hauled me from the car and took an intake of breath. I knew Eve as one of Karen's friends and when she was on a mission, there was no stopping her.

"Lord, what happened to you, Beth?" she asked.

"Er, coconut, morning..."

"Never mind, we haven't got time for this. You've an hour and a half before he has to be on set. Karen has reassured me you can do this. Don't mess it up. I should do this myself, but we're so short I'm taking on Jessie's and Marco's as it is," Eve said, marching me through a pair of double doors and down a long corridor to a dressing room. She knocked on the door, then breezed in and plastered a smile on her face.

"Oh Darling, Karen can't make it this morning, but not to worry, Beth's very competent." Her smile never wavered as she pointed a perfectly manicured fingernail at me and exited the door with a flourish and hissed, "Don't mess this up," before she left.

Briefly, our eyes met in the mirror's reflection before I felt a burn flash across my cheeks and lowered my head. God, it's him; Tom Austin, Hollywood A-lister and one hundred percent hunk. I held Karen's notes up to my face and made my way over to his dressing table. Once there, I put the notes down and pulled my hat down lower to cover my eyes. I glanced around the dressing room, which was smaller than I imagined. Decorated tastefully in taupe and creams with an impressive vanity table and highlighted mirror, a small wardrobe, and a single padded brown leather chair, as well as the one Mr Austin sat on. Reluctantly, I brought my gaze back to his.

"Good morning, Mr Austin. I'm here to do your face today. Are you allergic to anything?" I asked, trying not to scratch my face.

"No, unlike you, I don't suffer from hives," he said.

I watched his mouth curl up in one corner, unable to see the glint in his eyes with the hat pulled down; I wasn't sure if he was making fun of me.

"Karen always uses these products on my skin. There shouldn't be a problem as long as you apply them... correctly."

I felt a cold shiver race up my spine and a burst of heat flush through my face. Was that a warning? He's made a career out of playing the menacing sneer before wrecking vengeance on the baddies, but is that really necessary when speaking to a makeup artist? I gritted my teeth and turned my back on him. Right, let's get this done and get out of here.

When I next turned around, he had his eyes closed and his face perfectly relaxed. I stared a little, drinking in bone structure Adonis would kill for. His chiselled cleft chin, full lips, aquiline nose, and hewn cheekbones. Even his eyelashes and eyebrows framed those large, intelligent eyes better than the finest masterpiece. His brown hair shot through with hints of chestnut was divine, even his skin was without a blemish. I looked at his ears, hoping to find one bigger than the other or marred by a minuscule flaw, but no such luck.

Is it possible that I'd groaned in despair just looking at those impeccable features? One eye popped open and regarded me as though he was Smaug inspecting Bilbo Baggins when he tried to steal the Arkenstone. I watched the pupil dilate around what should have been an unremarkable ocean of blue, but his flared with islands of amber and brown.

My head lowered as I smoothed moisturiser over his skin, and the orb closed as his mouth dropped open with a soft, 'ah' sound. This dragon liked to be petted. Luckily for me, Karen and I had practised this look many times on each other and her nephews when they wanted to go to a fancy-dress party as Ironclaw. But working on the master canvas made my fingers tremor and throb as adrenalin sped its way through my blood like a flame travelling along the wick of a candle.

I've never worked on set before, but I knew time was critical, 'The Beauty Palace' where I normally work was pretty strict on time slots, but this was something else. It had to be camera ready and consistent from take to take. My breathing became erratic, as though it was the most difficult thing to do naturally.

My heart hammered in my chest, anticipating when I needed him to open his eyes again, and more of the shaky chemical flooded my bloodstream and turned my hands to jelly.

Both eyes popped open, and he regarded my fingers with a raised eyebrow and a drawn lip.

"Everything okay?" he said.

"Yes, almost done." I swallowed and drew my brush carefully under his eyelash. A spike of adrenalin sent my hand jolting up like a seismograph, dashing a fine cloud of powder into his eye.

He blinked rapidly and although his hand briefly hovered towards his face, like the professional he was, he held on to the instinct to rub the irritant away and waited for me to sort it out for him without ruining his foundation.

"Sorry," I muttered, dabbing at his face and wrestling the snake that my hand had become.

That dealt with, the only thing to do next was to add a wig and get the final okay from Eve.

"I'll need the lenses in today. Do you think you can do that?" he asked.

"Lens?" I swallowed hard.

"Yes, the black contacts, so I can really terrorise my antagonist."

"I don't think you'll need them," I muttered under my breath.

Oh god! Under the peak of my hat, I saw that gorgeous mouth widen and the full intensity of his smile sent a tremor equivalent to a force ten on the Richter scale through my body. However was I going to control my pinkie enough, not blind him trying to put the damn things in?

Balancing the tiny saucer of black on my index finger, it made its way to his face as though it were manoeuvring its way through a meteor shower. After I'd dropped the load twice, through gritted teeth, Tom's husky voice punched the air.

"Leave it! I'll do it myself."

I staggered backwards and bumped my hip on the dressing table hard, skittering bottles across the surface.

"Have you been drinking?" he asked sternly.

"No, not yet, but I intend to as soon as I get out of here." I turned my back and as I picked up the bottles, I heard a soft chuckle.

Eve entered the room, and I closed my eyes, expecting to hear a barrage of complaints as she examined my work.

After a silence that could have been hours but was probably minutes, she tapped my shoulder. "Not bad, pussycat." She turned from me and addressed Tom. "Darling, they're ready on set. We need you now."

"Considering, you did well, thanks. Better follow us through; there'll be touch ups to do," he added.

Shell-shocked, I trailed behind that impressive frame and powerful shoulders, feeling as though I might throw up at any second.

CHAPTER 2

BETH

Every day, for the next week, I got up at a whisper past midnight, and travelled to the studio to do Tom Austin's makeup. After my initial bumpy start, I saw little point in trying to impress him with my earth shatteringly ordinary looks. Instead, I concentrated on being as professional as I could be, while looking at a man who eighty percent of the world's population found attractive. Notice, I didn't say female. Yes, I'm not excluding a good percentage of men!

Although looks aren't everything, and in Tom's case that was true, even though he looked a million dollars, his personality was... shall I say – challenging. You know that dragon I mentioned earlier? Well, when he wasn't brooding, or growling, he was trying to set alight to things with his x-ray vision. Glaring at anyone who stepped out of line.

"You're late," he said as I rushed into his dressing room, my clothes plastered to my body as though they were a shower curtain clinging to my skin.

"The taxi had a puncture, and, lucky me, I found the only cabby in London who couldn't change a wheel," I said, taking off my overcoat and giving it a shake.

"And it's raining?"

I rolled my eyes at him. "No, I was so dirty after changing the tyre; I had a shower with my clothes on."

He cocked a lip at me, and a sparkle lit his eyes.

I frowned at him. "How come you're not wet? Doesn't it rain on A-listers?"

"Once you become really famous, you can purchase this app that puts an invisible shield over you in inclement weather. It's hellish expensive, but worth every penny."

I looked at his passive face without a hint of a smile and grunted. "Piss taker."

"You know, most women try to make themselves attractive around me, but you don't bother at all."

"Hmph, why would I when you're such a delight?" I pulled the hat I always wore when working here lower over my eyes. I knew I was nothing special to look at, as my previous boyfriend wouldn't go out with me unless I had my full face on. That was five years ago, and there was no way I'd let Tom know what I thought of him. "Perhaps I'm gay," I said.

He snorted.

"Or perhaps I don't find you attractive." I dried my hands on a towel and walked over to the dressing table.

"I would believe that, more than you're gay."

"Okay." I picked up the notes. "Not that it's any of your business, unless, of course, you're going to ask me out?" A grin pulled at my lips as I smeared moisturiser over his face.

He closed his eyes and laid his head back. "Perhaps I should. At least you wouldn't be high maintenance."

I chuckled. "Your current flame giving you trouble?"

He sighed. "Beautiful women aren't always worth the effort."

"That could be said about handsome men."

He opened one eye, and I tilted my head down. "What are you suggesting that I'm difficult?"

"I never said I found you attractive." I bit on my lip.

"Ah ha, that's true. Let's say you did. Would you find me hard work?"

I concentrated on his mouth as I smoothed foundation over his skin. "What a bizarre conversation we're having, Mr Rochester."

"Mr Rochester?" His hand shot out and grabbed my wrist. "Are you suggesting that I'm akin to the Mr Rochester in Jane Eyre?"

I focused on the fingers with a brush in them held captive by his hand. "Moody, grumpy, mysterious, glowering, now, why would you think I'd be referring to that Mr Rochester? Your characters are nothing alike."

His mouth pulled into a grim line, and I struggled to keep the grin from my face.

"Jane, you wouldn't be trying to besmirch my name, would you?"

"Why Sir, I would be afraid to. Least you set me ablaze with your fiery coals?"

"Fiery coals? I haven't got the black gaze of Mr

Rochester, and I seem to remember that Jane and he got married at the end of that book."

"Yes, they did, but it's fiction. Those things never happen in real life. And he was unfashionably rugged. They also never married until he had become horribly burnt and blinded in a house fire."

"I should be safe from marrying a plain Jane then."

"Heaven forbid a tragedy as great as that should befall someone as beautiful as you." I cleared my throat as the silence stretched between us. "Anyway, I didn't think you were the marrying kind. How old are you?"

"I'm not that old. I'm thirty-eight – ish," he replied.

I raised an eyebrow. Was that thirty-eight in actor's language? I wondered how long he'd been thirty-eight. "Exactly, you're a perpetual bachelor," I said, trying not to show how his gaze made my heart thump.

He shrugged. "I haven't found the right woman."

"You're too picky. But then you're like a kid in a sweet shop, who doesn't know which multi-coloured treat to choose."

"Thanks for that vote of confidence." He rumbled. "Anyhow, since you're not married, I don't think you can judge."

"Who says I'm not married?"

"You don't wear a ring," he said, pointing to his finger.

"Okay, you got me. But then I'm a lot younger than you and my choice compared to yours is equivalent to the school tuck shop."

"Perhaps you could make a bit of effort with your appearance?"

I grimaced as I brushed my hands down my sodden top and tried to pull the creases out.

"I had a good choice of sweets where I went to school. As a result, I was rather fat," he added.

I blinked and ran my gaze down his taut, muscular frame, and then nodded, not entirely sure whether we were talking about sweets or prospective partners, or whether he said that to make me feel better about being plain. Perhaps this dragon doesn't eat drab maidens?

"I gather you didn't go to an inner-city comprehensive."

He pursed his lips. "No, as you probably already know, I went to a private school, as a boarder."

"I didn't, but I guessed as much." I continued to apply his makeup and watched lines etch deep across his forehead. "Is it a sore point?"

"I feel I have to apologise for having a privileged upbringing," he said.

"Was it a privileged background the paparazzi alluded to or the fact your parents shipped you off to be rid of their fat, troublesome son?" I smiled as though I was an evil queen.

He winced. "You don't mince your words, do you? And going on that smirk you're wearing under that hat; you could easily be an assassin. My parents worked extremely hard to buy the best education they could afford for me and my five siblings."

"There's six of you?"

"Yes, five boys and a girl."

"Wow, no wonder your parents shipped you off to boarding school. There was only me and my brother, but my parents would have happily sent us to boarding school, if they could have. They often threatened it. Ah, but it couldn't have been that bad?"

"It wasn't. I had a very happy childhood."

I nodded. "If slightly overfed upbringing." I chuckled. Shaking my head at the thought of this man as a fat child.

"I've sorted that issue out now." He smiled, and I fixed my gaze on his chest and resisted the urge to touch him and see for myself how firm he was. "But the papers like to remind me I was a posh boy. I'm a posh man."

"I shouldn't worry about that. It works fine for Prince William. Anyhow, you're an actor. I'm sure you can rough it up when you need to."

"What was that governor? Give it some Jason Statham when I need to?" he said in a perfect cockney accent.

I smirked. "That was excellent. Bravo Mr Austin!"

He gave a little bow. "I'd like to be remembered for my acting skills, not my pretty face."

"You haven't got a pretty face." My feet shuffled as my gaze skittered off to study the door handle. "What I meant to say is, if you were around when Mr Rochester was alive, you'd fall into the unfashionably rugged camp too."

He lifted his eyebrow and gave me a grin as my face burned as though I'd sat in the sun too long. "Why Jane, was that a compliment you just gave me?"

"No, not really. How can you take credit for how you look? That was only down to genetics, or good genes. Now, if I'd told you that you're a great actor, then I would have given you a compliment."

He gave a dry little chuckle. "I couldn't agree with you more. Although, I'd like some credit for wrestling the puppy fat into muscle."

"Alright, I'll give you that. You look toned, and I do not know how much work it takes to achieve those results, but I'm guessing a lot."

CHAPTER 3

TOM

For the next fortnight, Jane came in every morning with a smile on her face, partly hidden by a variety of different hats, dressed like a psychedelic rainbow. There was something about her that brought out the devil in me. I was sure if I kept behaving like this, I'd grow horns and a pointy tail when she came near me. She just made me behave as though I'm free from the chains of decorum. I was a stallion, released in a field to kick my heels up and gallop around bucking and tossing my head.

One morning, I found myself hidden behind my dressing room door for ten minutes, waiting to jump out on her to see how she'd react, and she didn't disappoint me.

"AH! For the sake of shitake mushrooms!" Jane gasped as she did a convincing impression of Bambi skidding on ice through the door.

"Ha ha!" I laughed, grabbing her elbow to steady her. "What do mushrooms have to do with it?"

She turned around and glared at my chin. Itching to see her expression, I flipped her hat off and ducked my head.

17

But she was too quick and tucked her chin into her chest and, in one smooth move, grabbed her hat and plonked it on her head. "Mr Rochester, shame on you for divesting a lady of her hat and scaring her undergarments away!"

I laughed harder. "Very witty, Jane, and in a perfect period accent. Perhaps you ought to be an actress?"

"Ugh, no thank you. Can you imagine me in front of the lens?"

I looked at her half-hidden face and replied dryly, "Partly, yes."

"You idiot!" she said, tapping my arm. "In the chair, Mr Austin, and stop your Tom-foolery." She smirked.

"Pleased with yourself for that one, aren't you?" I glowered at her, then sat obediently in the makeup chair.

"Now I know why they named you Tom, you jester."

"What can I say? You bring out the stupid in me." I laid back in the chair and closed my eyes as she started massaging my face. "Ah, you have a wonderful touch, Jane. So relaxing. I think I'm going to need it this coming week. It's a tough one for Ironclaw, fraught with danger."

"Oh, and how much danger will Tom Austin be in?"

I sighed. "Minimal, I hope, but it's still going to be hard. I have two fight scenes, a chase on horseback and a perilous drop, as well as dodging arrows and thunderbolts, including a flight on a bad-tempered dragon."

"It doesn't sound that different from my week," she said.

I opened my eyes and watched as one side of her mouth quirked.

"So, are you one of these actors that does their own stunts?" she asked.

"Whenever they let me, yes. I don't want to do half a job, and I enjoy the physical challenge."

"Have you ever got hurt doing them?"

Her voice was softer now, and I wished I could see her eyes.

"Nothing too major, a concussion, a couple of cracked ribs, a broken finger, cuts and bruises, and a few serious dents to my ego. Other than that, I've been pretty fortunate."

She grimaced. "Please remember, I'm not a nurse. I can hide a bruise or two and disguise a cut, but broken bones or anything more serious. Well, you'll just have to avoid them."

I may not be able to see her expression, but with the pressure changing with each word as her fingers skated over my skin, it conveyed her feelings like a mute reading sign language. There was a contraction in my chest and my hand reached out and gave her fingers a squeeze. She startled like a flighty mare and froze.

"Don't worry Jane, I'll be careful."

She licked her lips. "Er, yes, I'm sure you will be. A man of your size has got to be hard to break."

"Hard, yes, but not impossible. Although, as you say, I'm pretty dense."

She picked up her notes and said, "Lucky you. You

start the day skin coloured," and flicking the sheet over, added, "Oh, but this afternoon you end up with purple eyes and a darkish scaly skin. That's going to take some time to pull off. It's going to be a really long day."

"Yes, a good twelve hours." I nodded in agreement.

"How do you fit a social life in with this kind of workload?"

"Well, I try not to, unless I'm already involved. That's why actors sometimes have long breaks between films."

"And sometimes they don't?" she asked.

"It's a fickle business. You never know when someone new is going to take the world by storm. Most actors are insecure and like to have the next project signed up well in advance." I gave her a wink. "And then, often working with a glamorous leading lady, leads to on set romance."

"I suppose that's bound to happen when you spend so much time in their company, and there's little time for anything else. But haven't you already mentioned you have a flame?"

"Yes, Alisha, my co-star from my previous movie."

She studied my face. "And how's that working out for you?"

I shrugged. "How long is it until we're finished here?"

"That good, huh? Just your wig to go."

"Good, I can't think about that now. I have work to do, Jane. You had better follow me out and don't blend into the distance. I want you to be watching carefully."

"As if I would?" She smirked. "Any reason in particular?" she asked.

"Yes, I want you to tell me how good an actor I am."

CHAPTER 4

TOM

Later that night, I opened the door to my Kensington apartment, and Drago, my American Leopard Hound, pounced on me.

"Whoa boy, did you miss me today? Who's a beautiful lad then? Have you had lots of playtime with Harry? Have you, have you?" I ruffled his coat, and was tempted to take him for a walk, but my legs ached and I just wanted to flop on the sofa for a while, let my bones soak into the soft pillows and close my eyes. Harry loved him to bits and came in three times a day, so I could guarantee he'd been for a long run with my ex-marine brother, probably around the entire park. After fifteen years in the forces, Harry retired and took up a dog sitting service for the rich and famous. He gets well paid, better than when he was risking life and limb for his country, and he kept ridiculously fit at the same time. Which made both him and his wife happy, as well as me and Drago.

"Did you go to Holland Park today?" I asked him as he skittered around my legs and licked my fingers.

Then I collapsed onto the settee, Drago jumped upon my chest and nuzzled my jaw, until I gave in and stroked his head. We laid in companionable silence, my mind drifting like a cloud as my brain slowly churned through the day. The morning had gone reasonably smoothly. Sitting in Jane's chair as she turned me into a purple scaled monster wasn't nearly as traumatic as being infected by a Cur Dragon's bite as my audience would expect. Quite the opposite, I was so relaxed she had to hold my head up by my hair as my chin kept hitting my chest. Apparently, I snored like a Furby. Now, no one's told me that before!

The afternoon was like one of those days where you wished you had turned over and gone back to sleep. Jake, playing a Mordork, slashed his sword with such enthusiasm he caught me once in the face and again in the stomach. I gasped and bent over double. Out of the corner of my eye, I watched Jane take a step forward. I couldn't imagine what she thought she could do as I gasped in a lungful of air, but through the haze of unshed tears I found a smile had crept onto my face. And when I went back to my chair for a touch up, her hands ghosted over me like a lover's kiss, and I sensed my shoulders softening against the seat.

From then on in, there was a mountain of retakes and problems with equipment, it felt as though we were in a pocket watch and the contents had sprung out all over the place, and however many hands tried to put it back together, it only made things worse.

At the end of the day, I slumped in the makeup chair while Jane removed the prosthetics and paint in silence. She took great care around the bruise appearing on my cheekbone, and as her fingers skated over my face, my eyes drifted closed.

"Next time, you'll have to duck," she said.

"Huh?" I roused myself.

"To avoid Mordork attacks. If Jake carries on like this, you're going to be black and blue. This is only day one of your *hard* week, and already you're sporting a bruise to your face and that punch to your stomach. Oof, it looked really painful. There, you're all done," she said, removing the cloth from my neck. "Please come to my chair at the end of tomorrow, not looking like you've been in a boxing match."

I watched as she chewed on her lip, rising from my seat, I smiled down at her. "The first day is always the worst. Don't worry, they will work out all the teething problems tomorrow." I grabbed her hand and gave it a squeeze as I left. She bit her lip as I walked away, and if I didn't know better, I would say an impish smile hovered around her mouth.

Through my half slumber daze, I heard the doorbell. Pushing Drago from my chest, I dragged myself to my feet and trudged over to the door.

"Alisha?" I said, opening the door.

"I thought you were going to call me?" She pouted and air kissed my cheeks as she made her way into the living room.

"Yeah, sorry. I haven't been in long. Today was a nightmare." I glanced at my watch and my eyebrows raised as I realised the hours had slipped away.

Drago made his way to his basket and lay down with a huff.

"What the hell's that on your cheek?" She giggled.

I put my fingers up to the bruise, feeling its edges. It didn't feel that bad.

"No, not just the bruise, the other thing."

I walked over to the living room mirror and glanced in it to study the bruise with a frown. "Jane." I smirked, looking at the bright green 'POW' sign and impact marks painted around the bruise. It looked like the cartoon captions used in Batman comics.

"Jane?" Alisha asked, sidling up to me and grabbing a handful of my goods.

"Yes, the makeup artist that's covering for Karen. She's a practical joker."

Alisha lifted her eyebrows at me and pursed her lips as she continued to massage my groin. "Do I need to be worried?"

"About plain Jane?" I snorted. "The ridiculous girl, who hides her face under a hat, and after a month, I don't even know her real name." I looked in the mirror and turned away from my reflection. Suddenly, my words had turned to ashes in my mouth and the handsome face no longer looked so appealing.

"That's alright then," Alisha said with a smile. "Since you're not taking me out tonight. You can entertain me another way."

For a moment, I was tempted to make an excuse and show her the door, but that would be a sinful waste of a decent hard on and a beautiful woman. So, I took her hand and led her to my bedroom.

Laying in what should have been post coital bliss. I found myself wide awake, thinking about Jane's impish smile and the heartless way I'd described her to Alisha. I glanced over to her, laid out like Sleeping Beauty in my bed, and thought about all the arguments we've had lately and how the best part of our relationship lay between the sheets. Once, that would have been enough, but now I longed for something deeper. Something like my parents shared.

I slipped out of bed and threw on some joggers and a t-shirt and, grabbing Drago's lead, made my way to the door. He was at my heels by the time I'd opened it, and we headed out into the night.

When we got back an hour later, Alisha was still asleep in my bed, and I quickly travelled through to the bathroom, showered and changed. And then made for the door, patting Drago on the head after filling his water bowl on my way to work. My brother would feed him, so there was no need to do anything else.

I was sipping a cup of green tea and eating a muesli bar by the time Jane entered the dressing room.

"That's yours." I said, pointing to a mug of tea sitting on my dressing table.

She paused en route, brushing leaves from her shoulders. "For me?" she asked. "It's drinkable, right? You haven't laced it with salt or chilli sauce or something?"

"As if I would?" I replied innocently. Her hat tilted. "Okay, so maybe I would, but not today. This is a peace offering," I added.

"A peace offering for what? Were you uncharitable about me when you found the POW sign I painted around your bruise?" She smirked.

I dropped my head, so she couldn't see the guilt painted on my face. "It made me laugh. I had no idea you had even done it. Although, with all the pranks I've played on you, I think I deserved it."

She tilted my head up and said, "Yes, I think you deserved it too, but if that's what it's going to do to you, I think I ought to stop."

"Why? What do you mean?"

"Tom, you look shattered. It's going to take a mountain of concealer to hide those dark circles."

"It wasn't your prank. I just didn't sleep well. I guess I was still buzzing after the long day's filming. Anyhow, I like our rapport. It's fun. I'm going to miss it when Karen comes back."

"Ah, but you'll have a prettier face to gaze at."

"Looks aren't everything," I muttered. Walking over to her, I picked off a few leaves and used my finger to tilt the brim of her hat back, but she tugged it down with her hands and took a step back. "I've got to ask. How did you get covered in leaves this morning?"

"Ah, wind," she said, nodding as if that explained everything.

"Wind? That's not an explanation. I never got covered in leaves when I arrived this morning."

"No, but then you have the fame app. I'm sure it works for windy days, dodging bird poo and leaves falling from trees as well as rain."

"Ah, yes. Now, why didn't I think of that before?" I asked.

"Well, no one said actors have to be intelligent. Although, under that pleasing exterior, I'm sure there hums a superior brain brimming with knowledge."

"Piss taker." I smirked, feeling a heaviness lift from my shoulders.

CHAPTER 5

BETH

Normally, I would have considered the week I've had as epic, but looking at Tom's, I felt I'd have to reassess it and class it as... meh, busy, trifling, staid, relaxing. I watched, my mouth agape, as he dragged himself free of a muddy pool, and staged a fight with three men dressed in leathery armoured costumes and bulbous headwear, resembling some ghastly giant insect. Apparently, they couldn't see well out of their headgear, so Tom's body sustained a fair amount of contact. He took every blow, with a stoic acceptance, followed by a good amount of back patting.

Then there was a love scene, which caused my heart to squeeze, followed by more fighting, a flight on an imaginary dragon, where he hung upside down in a harness for three hours, which looked really uncomfortable around the nether regions. And then back in a pool to film underwater sequences.

While he waited for another actor to play their part or adjustments to the set, he was doing sit-ups, press-ups or lifting weights. Or failing that, eating. This man ate a lot, but then he had a furnace that was continually running at full steam.

How he managed a social life after this was mind-boggling. When I got home, I just wanted to lie in front of the telly or read a good book until I chilled out enough to fall into bed and catch a few hours before the madness started again.

When I thought back to his evasiveness around his relationship, I guessed not everything could be plain sailing when he juggled so many balls. On the surface, he could appear surly and dark, but underneath there was a clown, a joker, a man looking for approval. Perhaps even normality? A man who wanted people to see through the beautiful exterior to the depths beneath, and prove to the world that he wasn't just a handsome face. So, he pushed himself far beyond what most people could achieve. Despite that, it was never enough.

Did he judge everyone else by his own high standards? Was that why his relationships failed? Was beauty a curse? I would never know, but I suspected it caused as many problems as being forgettable did.

When I first met him, his looks floored me. Now

I wanted to explore the contents of this very attractive parcel as the ribbons and bows lay forgotten on the floor at my feet. The presents, wrapped up in brown paper, barely hinted at the treasures within. Yet, as I uncovered another layer, as though he was some magical Russian doll, my hands shook, eyebrows raised, and I itched to reveal more.

When he fell asleep, sitting in my chair as I touched up his makeup or changed his face into one of the many characters needed to play Ironclaw. I flittered around him like an oxpecker cleaning ticks from an African beast. Mr Austin, like Mr Rochester, might seem to be untouchable on the first encounter, but both men liked a soothing touch. When he closed his eyes and his head nodded, a flutter of pride sparked to life in my chest – I knew he needed these brief moments of calm to maintain the ferocious pace he demanded of himself.

Come Friday night, he returned to my chair positioned behind the cameras in the bowels of the studio, as the set emptied of crew and the myriad members of film staff left for the evening. He sat down heavily and scowled.

"Jane," he growled. "Have you eaten?"

"No, not yet. We're two staff members short today, so I'm covering for them."

He grunted. "Your hands are shaking. You need to eat for heaven's sake!"

I looked at him. "What are you so grouchy about?"

"Someone with your track record of disasters can't go around neglecting themselves." His eyes burned darkly at me.

I smiled. "You don't need to worry about me, Sir. I can look after myself."

"Huh, I have seen no evidence of that."

I smoothed his face with cleansing lotion and watched his features slacken.

"Well, as soon as your makeup is off, I'm going to the pub for dinner."

One of his eyes cracked open. "Oh, who are you going with?" he asked.

"The rest of the makeup team. We've all been so busy we thought we'd treat ourselves. Anyhow, it's Friday night and Marco and I often go for a drink together. I think Karen's going to join us, too."

He closed his eye. "So, you and Marco are friends? Just friends or something else?"

"We get on well, yes." I watched his mouth tighten, and I felt a bubble tickle my chest. My mouth quirked at the corner.

"Well, what is he to you?"

My smile broadened. "He's a special friend."

Both his eyes opened, and I tilted my head down. "You're teasing me, Jane?"

"About what, Mr Rochester?" I asked, wide-eyed.

"You always call me Mr Rochester when you're hatching something," he said, giving me a suspicious look.

"Why should you worry if Marco and I are dating?" I shuffled my feet and entwined my fingers.

"You're acting nervous, Jane," he huffed. "Why can't you tip that blasted hat back, or leave it off altogether? It makes it nearly impossible to tell what you're really thinking."

I smiled. "I like my hat, and the fact you can't read my expression. Anyway, back to the subject we're discussing. Marco is cute and kind of funny. We rub along nicely."

"Does that mean you're dating him?" He sat upright and took hold of my wrist.

"Why do you care who I date? You have your beautiful, film star actress to go home to. A matching pair of figurines that complement each other beautifully."

"Huh, what utter rubbish you're talking. It takes more than the exterior to find your perfect match." He ran a hand through his hair. "And Marco isn't yours."

"How do you know that?" I asked, straightening my shoulders.

"He's the least exciting guy there is."

My mouth dropped open. "Tell me, how did you come to that conclusion? He has blue spiky hair, a ring through his nose and a tongue stud."

"He's overcompensating for a lack of personality."

I put my hands on my hips. "Really? Have you actually spoken to him, because if you had, I'm sure you'd find out he is just as interesting on the inside as the outside?"

He waved his hand dismissively and then focused his gaze as though he were listening for a pin to drop and had to know the location. "How do you know he has a tongue stud?"

I rolled my eyes under my hat and pursed my lips, but his face remained unyielding, as if it was made of granite. I considered telling him you can see it when he talks, but that unmoveable stubborn jaw made me dig my heels in and wave a riding crop in his face. "Well obviously, I could feel it when he licked the shell of my ear the other night." My eyes widened as I watched his face pale.

"He did no such thing!" The silence stretched between us. "I hope he took you out for dinner first. I presume you won't be doing that again. Putting out on a first date never works.

My mouth dropped open. "I would say that *you* are the one being presumptuous. What I do, with whoever I like, is none of your business! Good night, Mr Austin and I hope you have a wonderful evening playing cribbage with Alisha."

"Jane...?"

"There's no one called Jane here," I said, gritting my teeth as I strode away.

CHAPTER 6

TOM

As Jane's diminutive figure left the building, my lips formed into a tight line. I got out of the chair and threw the towel from around my neck to the floor and stood for a moment, glaring at the studio door as it closed behind her. Sensations boiled inside me like an angry snake, fangs sharp as daggers, ready to strike. I wanted to punch something or stride after her and grab her arm, swing her around so she faced me, and knock that monstrous hat from her head.

I wanted answers, but as my anger ebbed, I wondered what I wanted answers to, and whether I had any right to demand them of her. I'd never acted this way before, as though I were a grizzly bear awoken months too early from winter hibernation, to find I wore a tutu and was surrounded by a performing circus held in my honour. A frown deepened across my forehead, and I shook myself. Something alien stirred within my breast, lighting a flame to my anger. Only I swear this fire burned green, not red. I turned on my heel and strode in the opposite direction to the conundrum that made me act, a cross between a gyroscope spinning out of control and a lion soothed by a magical potion.

"Jane," I sighed to myself. "No, you're right. That isn't your name. Any more than I'm Mr Rochester. Austin, you're a fool! It was you who behaved badly, your anger totally misplaced. It should not be towards her, or that pimped up parrot she might be seeing. You have only yourself to blame." I walked across the dim, echoing set and waved good night to the cleaner on my way out.

Back home, Drago met me with a wag of his tail, so I grabbed his lead and was about to head out when Alisha greeted me as I opened the door.

"Where are you going?" she asked with a frown faintly pulling at her brow.

"Out. Drago needs a walk. Do you want to come with me?"

I watched as a debate raged over her face. Alisha wasn't an animal lover, which was another reason I never thought it could work between us. I had been raised among the fields and meadows of Kent, and lived in a large house with horses, dogs, geese, cats, and rabbits. Why should I imagine, it would work out with someone who hated having a hair out of place, let alone a stray one on her skirt? Am I so superficial that I only go for looks? And chemistry? There certainly was a magnetic sexual chemistry between us. But would I class her as a friend? Even my best friend? My mother always said Dad was her best friend, the person she could rely on one hundred percent. And Dad, when I asked, what made a successful relationship always replied. "Teamwork, Tom. There's no other way."

She took hold of Drago's lead and tugged him back into my apartment and closed the door behind us, so we stood in the hallway toe to toe.

"I missed you, Tom. You're so busy filming Ironclaw, I'm feeling quite neglected." She brushed my groin, her eyes flashing. "Don't you need a workout? I'm sure I can help with all that pent up energy."

I leant forward and kissed her full lips. Oh, hell, why did I keep doing this? By the time we were back inside, making our way to my bedroom, Drago had made himself comfortable in his bed. He lifted his eyes as I glanced over. A pang of guilt speared me as I saw the resignation in his face, but it didn't stop me.

Could Jane be right, that Alisha and I are a matching pair of ornamental figurines? Pretty to look at and seemingly a pair, but inside, one made of porcelain, the other clay, and both hollow inside? Not that she had suggested that - Jane was honest but never cruel. If I was with someone like Jane, would Drago get his walk and me my oats?

I paused by my bed, suddenly torn between lust's primeval need and Jane's tight shoulders as she strode away from me, to Drago's look of disappointment that he wouldn't get a walk.

Alisha, sensing the change, undid my trousers and dropped to her knees. Moments later, I hadn't a thought in my head. Standing with my eyes closed, I didn't see the smug smile curving her lips, her mouth full of the piece of my body that rendered me brainless. But after we had finished, the anxiety crept back, gnawing like a mouse trapped between the joists. I had to know she wasn't upset with me. So, when Alisha was in the bathroom, I scribbled her a note. Picked up Drago's lead and headed out. Pounding the pavements, I made my way to the dog friendly pub I knew she would be having dinner in.

When I got there, I glanced at my phone and hovered outside the doors, listening to the hum from inside - the laughter and chatter. Would she be among friends, happy and smiling, and me forgotten, pushed from her mind, like a dirty piece of clothing at the back of a wardrobe? My gaze watched the shadows dance across the imperfect squares of glass, some vividly coloured in blues and reds, which only reminded me of how Jane dressed to disguise herself.

I looked down at Drago and he wagged his tail, pushed his nose towards the door and snuffled the plethora of scents invading his nostrils. Whatever he had smelt made him lean forward, tightening his leash until he'd almost dragged me indoors.

CHAPTER 7

BETH

"Stubborn, impossible, interfering man!" I said as I walked the long stretch between studio lots towards the main gate. In the distance was a group hovering by the exit, but I was in no hurry, and they weren't waiting for me anyhow. I could see the bob of Marco's hair halfway between me and the others. He gave them a wave, and they cheered.

One thing Tom was right about was that Marco wasn't for me. He wasn't boring, and although we often went to the pub together, he'd drop me like a stone whenever a whiff of a semi-attractive female came his way. If he were a horse, they would put him out to stud. The guy had one thing on his brain, and he wasn't too fussy about how or who he got it from, just that he got it.

Inevitably, he'd tried to get me into his bed. Well, I'd be optimistic if I thought we would get that far, but I'm a relationship girl. There must be an emotional connection before anyone sees the colour of my knickers. That's just how I am. And that's the great thing about Marco. He doesn't care that I turned him down. He's like margarine on bread, he just lies down and takes life whichever way it's spread – always with a smile on his face and an eye on the next skirt that walks in.

I think that's why he became a makeup artist. In an industry full of gay men and women co-workers, he couldn't lose. If he wasn't working with women, he was making them look more beautiful.

By the time the crowd at the gate had dispersed, I had replaced the anger I felt towards Tom with a peculiar type of affection. Although Marco hadn't worked directly with Tom, he had been on the set long enough for his reputation as a womaniser to spread through the cast. The way Tom reacted may have come across as overbearing or even condescending, but with hindsight, I pictured him as a large black raven pecking a threat away from his egg with a sharp beak. Funny, to think of myself as his egg, but, even in the little time I'd known him, I sensed his instinct was to shuffle me under his wing and tidy stray feathers.

By the time I pushed the pub doors open, I had a wry smile dancing around my mouth.

"You look happy," a familiar voice said as the door

swung shut behind me.

"Karen, it's so good to see you!" I pulled her in for a hug.

"I texted you every week, chick," she said, handing me a drink.

"Yeah, I know, but it's not the same. I need a proper catch up. How's your arm?"

Karen flexed her fingers. "Pretty good, darling, and I've missed you, too."

Since her break, Karen had been 'convalescing' in the South of France with a 'friend'. I joked with her that she sounded like a high-flying call girl when she told me she was going to Monaco to entertain an old client of hers.

She had slapped my arm and winked. "He *was* an old client of mine. I can't tell you much, apart from I used to do his stage makeup before he became mega famous and turned his hand to producing."

Apparently, he was staying in his luxury villa overlooking the city so he could have an eagle-eyed view of the Grand Prix and when he heard about her fall, had invited her out there.

"I knew we had a connection," she'd told me, "because when I gave him a spray tan, something came up."

It took me a minute for the penny to drop and then I hooted like a train. "And you've stayed 'friends' ever since? Why is it I've never heard mention of him before?" Karen and I had been friends for six years and I thought I knew all her boyfriend's past and present.

"You have heard of him, but not under his real name. He was kind of married at the time, and so big in Hollywood that everything had to be kept hush-hush."

"How could he have been kind of married?" I'd asked.

"Well, in the public eye, they were Hollywood's dream team. In private, they lived their own lives. You know how it is, appearances are everything in Tinsel town."

I'm still not sure who this person is, but the way she's kept his name a secret all these years says a lot about how she feels for him.

"So, you're back at the studio next week?" I asked as we finished our hug and made for a padded bench by the bar. Marco asked us whether we wanted a drink before we went through to our table. As we were early, we both said we would and took a moment to catch up.

"Yes, I'm back on Tuesday. I have a meeting with Eve first thing on Monday morning. Eve's been chirping like a canary over your work. I think I may have to kill you off to stop the competition, otherwise I'll blink, and you'll take my place."

I chuckled

"Anyway, what was it like working with the guy you've drooled over for years?" she asked, wrapping an arm through mine.

'Terrifying,' I thought. "Unbelievably, he's better looking in reality and incredibly intimidating first off, kind of growly and aloof." She nodded in agreement. "But apparently he's also got a sense of humour." My face heated thinking about all the times he tried to make me jump or pretended I'd stabbed him with a brush, relishing my reaction like a naughty schoolboy.

"Really? I can't say I've noticed." She gave a little shrug and grinned at me. "What's with the bright clothes and hat?"

"It's camouflage. After the first day we met, I didn't see the point of getting all dressed up for work at the witching hour to impress someone who would never look at me romantically, and is completely out of my league, first impressions and all that."

"Oh Beth, you don't give yourself enough credit."

"I would say, I'm realistic. You saw the photo of how I turned up the first day. I think the taxi driver disinfected his cab after I got out! And Tom's an A-list star, who's looks are a 10 plus and I'm a, currently out of work makeup artist, who is a 7 with a lot of effort."

"You're a 7 without the effort." She smirked.

"See, even you can't help being truthful! And I'm a go steady girl, not a one-night stander," I said, sipping my drink.

She nodded and asked, "You're not going back to the

Beauty Palace, are you?"

"I thought about it, but the one thing this has shown me is that I'm stuck in a rut. I think it's about time I spread my wings a little."

"So, what's your next move?"

"I'm not sure. You'll have to watch this space. Enough about me. What happened in Monaco?"

"I made pole position."

I nudged her arm, and we grinned at each other.

"The table's ready," Marco called, and we all traipsed into the restaurant part of the pub.

An hour and a half later, we emerged from the restaurant, our bellies full and surrounded by a hazy, giggly booze induced bubble. I made my way straight to the bathroom and as I washed my hands, I stared in the mirror. For a second, I pictured Tom stood behind me like a dark angel with a set of midnight wings looming over his shoulder. The thought of this man standing watch over me made my heart pound in my chest. Who wouldn't want Ironclaw, the protector, watching over them? Running a finger down the column of their neck and guiding them around by those strong elegant fingers to come face to face with the most exquisite angel of them all?

Before my imagination could take me any further, I shook my head and plonked my hat back on my head. I hadn't worn it while we were in the restaurant, but just the mirage of Tom's ghost standing behind me made me don it as if it was a magical invisibility cloak.

As I exited the ladies, a figure pushed through

the pubs doors and my pulse thundered in my ears. Instinctively, I dropped my head and focused on the unusual looking dog at his feet. The dog raced in my direction as if it was following the scent of a squirrel up a tree.

"Shit, what's he doing here?" I muttered under my breath as I squeezed myself into the booth beside Karen.

"Look who it isn't, Beth," she said, nudging me in the ribs. "Darling, come and join us!" she called to him.

The crowd we were with followed her words as though they were watching a tennis match at Wimbledon, shortly followed by the rest of the pub. There was a flurry of women making a grab for their handbags to check out their makeup and wipe the drool from their lips, and one or two men so drawn to him they looked like they had an invisible hula hoop gyrating their hips.

Tom's dog sat obediently at the end of the table; he craned his neck until his nose grazed my trousers. I did a mental check to see if I had anything worth his interest in my pockets. I didn't, but as I gazed into his mismatched adoring eyes and reached out to coax his spotty, grey, black, and golden coat, I couldn't think of a better dog to be Tom's.

"Wow, you're a beautiful boy, aren't you?" I said.

"Thanks very much," Tom said drily, as he tugged a chair over to the end of the table and sat down.

"Not you, you fool."

"Oh, were you talking about my dog?"

"Yes." I glanced around the pub and wondered how many people that nodded their heads in agreement to my statement weren't referring to his dog. "Well, you're beautiful, aren't you?" I hoped the dim lighting hid the flush creeping up my neck.

"His name's Drago. Mine's Tom if you want to try it out?" he said.

"I know your name. Everyone in this pub knows your name and probably more intimate facts about your life than your mother."

"Thanks for that reminder," he said, shuffling into his seat.

I smirked. "What type of dog is he? Did you have him bred specially to suit you?"

"I guess you're not cross with me anymore since you're back to your playful self?"

"How could anyone stay mad at you, Mr Rochester? What type of dog is he?"

"Hey Tom, can I have your autograph?" A burly hand, smothered in tattoo's pushed a beer mat under his nose.

"Sure," he said, taking hold of the stained mat.

"To Kathy. That's my Misses. She reckons you've got rock hard buns and wouldn't mind a handful."

Tom raised an eyebrow and signed with a flourish. "He's an American Leopard hound. I got him when I was working in the States, from a rescue when he was a puppy."

"Darling, shuffle along so I can speak to Tom." Karen said, giving me a nudge from behind.

I scootered over to the next seat. A ragged line of

fans had formed by the time Karen had taken my seat. Drago inched his way towards me and wedged his nose in my crotch. His forgive me eyes made me melt, and I ruffled his coat and told him what a good boy he was.

Mack, the landlord, came over and bellowed at his regulars. "Alright, alright, I know we have a celebrity in our midst, but there's no need to crowd the poor fella! He's been here before, and he'll come again if you don't harass him too much." Turning to Tom, he said, "Bleedin' heck, you've got more interest than the crown jewels. Sit down and leave your scraps of paper at the bar. Mr Austin 'ill sign them at his leisure and stop thieving me bleedin' bar mats. I'll be charging for them, and they won't be bloody cheap, either!"

Reluctantly, the crowd dispersed as Tom nodded in thanks to the landlord.

I concentrated my attention on Drago, who was lapping it up, while I kept an ear open, listening to Tom and Karen's conversation. Oddly, they talked about everything but work. Tom knew Monaco well, and by the way he spoke, he knew exactly who her mystery man was.

I looked at Karen, dressed in peacock blue and shimmering with exotic brilliance, even in my bright colours. I was a dowdy brown bird in comparison. I guessed it shouldn't have smarted that Karen had kept that part of her life a secret from me, but as she told Tom her deepest secrets, it was evident he knew all about their relationship, even though I wasn't aware they were even friends, but it did. How did the saying go - birds of a feather flock together?

Marco came over to them. "Hey Tom, would you like

a drink? We can't have you sitting there stone cold sober when the rest of us are three sheets to the wind."

"I don't usually drink," he said.

"Well, this isn't usual. This is an unusual situation, and you've a day off tomorrow." Marco grinned engagingly.

"Alright, I'll have one."

"Okey dokey, what's your poison?"

Tom grimaced. "Whatever you're having, as long as it's not a pint. I must head home soon. I only came here to speak to Jane."

"Okay mate. Whoever Jane is?" Marco muttered, weaving his way to the bar.

Both mine and Drago's ears pricked up. "Tom came to speak to me?" I asked his dog. "What about?" Strangely enough, Drago didn't have an answer.

By the third round, Tom had his wallet out and had brought everyone in the bar a drink. He lounged with a smile on his face, his elbows resting on a sticky patch on the counter.

I collared Marco, on his way to a brunette with her hair in a bun and glasses on. "What did you give him to drink?" I asked.

"It was some 'ery good wodka," he said, slapping his chest as though he was Ivan Simeonov in RED. "It vill put hair on vis chest. Make a man of vim!"

I narrowed my eyes at him. "How strong? You've remembered; he rarely drinks?"

"Ah, don't vorry vittle lady. It vas 'ery good stuff, make vim into a man! Excuse me beautiful lady, I must conquer that office queen over vere, pull the pins from her vair and vatch it tumble down her back, do svidaniya!" He staggered off in the woman's direction. I watched as they greeted each other with a kiss on both cheeks and then left arm in arm.

"Was Marco speaking Russian?" Karen asked.

"Apparently so. He's a man of many talents. One of them being getting Tom drunk after three glasses."

"Of what?" Karen frowned.

"Some special Russian vodka." I nodded towards a fancy bottle at the bar.

"Vodka, I thought he was drinking water!"

"So did he, seeing how quickly he necked it," I said with a smirk.

Tom came back to join our table with a man I'd never met before. Although I thought he was a regular since he was friendly with the landlord.

Drago put his paw on my knee, and I continued to stroke him.

"Terry, these are my friends, Karen, Jane... where's the parrot?" He looked around him as if Marco would materialise if he kept looking.

"Marco left," I replied, grinning.

"Left? When?" he asked, leaning into the table.

"When you were at the bar."

"Did he fly off?" Terry asked with a cocky smirk. "Did

you bring a dog and a parrot with you?"

"No, just a dog. His name's Drago," Tom said.

"Looks like your dog has the hots for her. Hey, what's your name, luv?" he asked me.

"Jane," Tom answered.

"You've pulled. He's got his lipstick out." Terry slapped his knee and snorted with laughter.

My hands froze on Drago's coat, and I wrapped my hand around his lead and lowered my beetroot-coloured face.

"I'd have my lipstick out too, if Jane had been stroking me all night." Tom insisted. "She has wonderful hands."

"She'd have to have something. She looks like a cross between Madonna and Coco the Clown!"

I prayed for a hole to open up beneath my chair as the pub erupted in laughter.

"Hey, that's my friend you're talking about!" Tom grabbed the man's shoulder and glared at him.

Karen took hold of my hand and gave it a squeeze. "Do you want to leave?"

"Please don't say anything else," I pleaded with Tom.

Drago had the best idea; he pulled me to the door and then Tom said it.

"I'd happily get my kit off for Jane. Looks aren't everything you know!"

I didn't hear anymore. Drago pulled me through the double doors so fast, I thought I was a cannon ball launched from a ship. He took me to the first lamppost and cocked his leg. Had he been that desperate to go? By the look on his face, I would never have thought so. If it's possible for a dog to wear an expression of disdain, I'd say Drago wore it.

Whether he was picturing Terry or Tom as the lamppost, I couldn't have said for sure.

CHAPTER 8

TOM

"What?" I looked at Karen's face, scrunched up as if she was about to throw a punch.

"If I hadn't just got this working again, I'd hit you right now!" she said, flexing her hand.

"What? I'm not ashamed of my body."

There were cheers all around us: "get them off, get them off!"

I frowned. What was happening?

"Of course, you're not ashamed of your body, Mr Bloody Perfect. But your body wasn't the one in question. It was Jane's. I mean Beth's."

"Who's Beth?" My addled brain wasn't keeping up.

"One more word from you and I'll take the risk and smack some bloody sense in that faultless face of yours."

I opened my mouth.

"Don't! We're leaving. Even your dog has more sense," Karen said.

Grabbing my arm and dragging me to my feet. I nodded and waved at my new friends as I left the bar.

And then the air hit me, and my senses pinged into sharp relief.

"Jane, where's Jane? I came here to apologise."

"Well, you did a spectacularly grand job of that!" She narrowed her eyes. "What did you do that warranted an apology?"

I ran a hand through my hair. "Nothing that bad, considering what I've just said." I spotted Jane by a lamppost and made my way over. Drago saw me coming and turned his back on me and sat down.

"I'm so sorry that came out all wrong," I said as I approached her.

"It wasn't really your fault."

I had expected an attack, anger, or at least sharp words, but she didn't even look mad. More resigned, just like Drago had when I hadn't walked him and took Alisha to bed instead. Alisha, I'd forgotten all about her.

"It was Terry who did the insulting. You only tried to defend me."

"Well, I shouldn't have mentioned my lipstick or that I'd get my kit off."

"Because I have wonderful hands." She smirked and gave me a nudge. "I'm sure you look good naked."

I shrugged. "I'm surprised you haven't seen me. Everyone else has on set."

"Lucky them."

"Next time I have to get my kit off for a scene, you'll be the first to know."

"That's friendship for you. Let the plain friend ogle your body for free!"

"I don't think you're plain, but I'd like to think we're friends."

"Here, have Drago back, I think you're in the doghouse," she said.

I rolled my eyes. "I think I'm in everyone's doghouse, but as long as I'm not in yours."

"Well. I haven't got enough friends to be that picky. And now there's the promise of you get your kit off. So, meh, I'll forgive you this time for being an appalling drunk."

"Thanks. Why do you think I rarely touch the stuff?"

"Well, I thought it was because alcohol is full of sugar, but having experienced you in action - I'd just say you can't handle your drink."

I smirked. "I guess you're right. See you on Monday?"

She laid her fingers on my jaw and I sighed, then tapped my face and smiled.

"I'll look forward to seeing you on Monday, buns of steel." She joked.

I wiggled my bum. "If you're good, I'll let you have a feel." Then bit my lip. I guess the alcohol was still controlling my mouth.

"Never mind feeling it, I'll be painting it grey if you've a scene coming up."

Her cheeks flushed under the streetlight. She walked back to Karen, and I watched as they got into a cab. I found myself grinning as I walked Drago home.

"Where the hell did you disappear off to?" Alisha asked the second I walked in the door.

"I left you a note," I said, calmly hanging Drago's lead up as I ran a hand down his back and stroked his ears.

"You expect me to believe you walked that bloody mutt for three hours?" She pointed at Drago as he skulked into his basket.

"I met a friend," I said, turning my back on her and throwing my keys on a table.

"In the pub? You wreak of booze! I thought you didn't even drink."

"I don't, usually," I said. Toeing my trainers off.

"That's just typical of you! You selfish bastard! Whenever I want to go out, you're too tired, but you'll walk that," she said, pointing to Drago, "at any bloody hour!"

I stood looking at her. My temper was like the slow march of molten flow making its way down a hillside. "Yes, you're right, I haven't been fair. I walk Drago when I can't sleep or if something's on my mind." My heart pummelled against my chest. I was finally going to do it – break the chains that had been slowly tightening around me the last month. "And I am selfish. When I'm on set, that's all I can focus on. Having a relationship when I'm so busy is a recipe for disaster. You deserve someone who puts you first, and that isn't me..."

She stepped towards me and kissed my mouth, silencing my words. I kissed her back, then pulled away. "I can't keep doing this," I said. "I don't want to."

Her hand went to my chest and trailed down my body. She grabbed a handful. I closed my eyes. Feeling it swell as she massaged my groin. Nausea enveloped me. "Make it up to me," she purred.

My eyes opened and dropped to Drago's. "No, I'm sorry I ca..." I stepped away, resisting the urge to push her from me.

She pushed her finger towards my face and then walked to the door. "Later, when you're sober, we'll talk."

I wanted to say, what's the point of talking when it's over, but she had already left.

Looking at the closed door, I punched the air. I might have even done a little hop. Drago cocked his head to one side and then his tongue flopped out of his mouth. I whistled as I entered my bedroom. One whiff of Alisha's perfume and I grabbed a pillow out of the closet and made my way back into the lounge.

"Fancy a snuggle?" I asked Drago, as I made myself comfortable on the sofa. I grabbed a rug and made him a bed beside me. He jumped up and laid down, nestled against my stomach. I wrapped an arm around him and closed my eyes. "It's just you and me, kid," I said, falling asleep.

***

It's unusual during filming to have two consecutive days off, especially when Ironclaw is so close to completion and it's the weekend. No, that's not quite right, most actors aren't needed every day, but when you are the lead, it's much more demanding and I was knackered. My body ached in places I never knew existed and, however much I enjoyed doing my own stunts, this series had been hard. The Mordork cast was taking great pains to make their fight scenes authentic, and my body was littered with the evidence of their ambition.

When I got out of the shower on Sunday morning and looked at my physique in the mirror, over the sculpted contours of my abs and my solid pectorals, I could honestly say I was in the best shape of my life. But mentally, and somewhere deep in my marrow, something laid heavy as if I wore a leaded suit of armour. But somehow, when Jane was near, the plated metal floated free. The more I experienced it, the more I wanted to substitute the weight for the lightness. How one person could have such a profound effect, I couldn't say, but with Jane around I didn't just enjoy stories of knights of old and mythical beasts. I believed in them.

As I replayed the conversation I'd had with Jane, my lips curled as I thought of ways that would make her flush, laugh, and curse me at the same time. I whistled to Drago, grabbed his lead off the side, and went in search of a little gift that would act as well as any whoopie cushion.

CHAPTER 9

TOM

On Monday morning, I watched my dressing room door with a combination of fascination and amusement. Every morning Jane entered dressed in an outfit more outrageous than the last. Usually, a cross between something Vivienne Westwood or a tramp might wear. Her more stylish outfits were often decorated by her latest disaster; the taxi's flat, the coffee someone bumped into her with in the corridor, or the 'lucky' bird poo that splattered her on the way in. This woman was a magnet for the bizarre and wayward encounter. It was like watching a comedy skit, and I found my mouth turning up in anticipation of the latest episode.

The more Jane and I spoke, the more I felt as if I was revealing a canvas buried by a mountain of grime and unfavourable viewing. Whether, when all the debris was removed, it would reveal a masterpiece, I wasn't sure, and I was beginning not to care. It was so much fun peeling off the layers; I didn't want to stop.

It's odd. I knew her name wasn't Jane, but somehow, I couldn't recall her ever telling me her real one, and now Jane had become ingrained so deep in my psyche I couldn't imagine her as anything else. Did that make me

Mr Rochester? Probably not. I go for exotic butterflies that dazzle with their vibrant colours and eye-catching wings, but if you asked me what Jane looked like, I wouldn't be able to tell you anything for sure. I haven't seen her face in its entirety, only snapshots of her chin, a flash of blue eyelash or brown. She could be a dowdy peahen or a spectacular peacock, probably the former, though, otherwise she would bask in the sun, dazzling passersby with her riotous colours against the blank background of a rock.

"Jane," I said, as she tumbled into the dressing room. "We have a busy day. I have to emerge from a swamp and fight a Mordork to the death. It's a difficult encounter, and it'll take its toll on Ironclaw. I'll need you to be constantly on hand to touch up and rework my face."

"Yes, I know. I had a two-hour meeting with the rest of the makeup department yesterday. Are they starting with the swamp scene?" she asked, disentangling a reel of cotton from the heel of her shoe.

I watched with an upturn to my lips as she tugged on the thread and part of her hem released.

"How did you manage that?" I asked.

She shrugged her shoulders. "Who knew I lifted my foot that high when I walk?"

"Who knew indeed?" I turned back to the mirror as I watched the creases around my eyes deepen. "Yes, they're starting with the swamp scene." I undid my shirt and slipped it off my shoulders.

"What are you doing?" Her mouth dropped open as her body snapped upright.

"Undressing, ready for my full body makeup. I've got to match. Can't have me coming out of the swamp naked, with a grey head and skin coloured body. That wouldn't be realistic at all."

"Naked?"

"Haven't you done a spray tan before?"

"Yea… yes, but I thought the rest of the cast got their body paint in a booth."

"Well, Karen always worked her magic in here. So, I thought we'd carry on, and I promised you Saturday night."

I watched as she bit her lip and tilted her head down, so I could only see the top of her hat.

"Is that a problem?" I asked, imagining a flush of colour spread over her cheeks.

Her head tilted to one side, and she straightened her shoulders. "No. No problem at all. Get your kit off and I'll start on your face." She raised her head, and I saw the beam of her smile peeking out from under the brim of her hat.

I undid the button and slipped my pants and trousers off in one go, then stood upright and placed my clothing neatly on the spare chair. Then sat down and crossed my leg over my knee and waited. I noticed her swallow hard before she headed over to me, and my smile deepened. I would have loved to see her eyes widen as she tried not to look in my lap, but I was sure she'd keep her head down and avoid my face. Of course, this focused her gaze just where I wanted it, and I, like the ten-year-old boy who'd put a snake in his teacher's bed, couldn't wait for her reaction.

"Parlour games, Mr Rochester," she said as she made her way over to me and lent against my shoulder. "I've seen bigger snakes."

I chuckled and looked at the knitted snake sock my penis was wearing. "But none as colourful as this one."

"Well, that's one more thing you have in common with Mr R. He liked to disguise himself and play tricks on his guests." She grinned at me.

"Do you like the colour? I thought of you when I bought it."

Her mouth opened. "What are you insinuating about me, that I'm colour blind? After all, red, purple and green should never be seen."

"Don't forget the orange. And I'm sure you've worn something similar before."

"You jest, sir. I have never worn a penis sock in my life. Having that manly appendage missing from my body, I have no use of one."

I smirked at her. "I'm very glad to hear that, Jane. Although you camouflage your true self well, I'm glad you don't disguise it so well I can't tell what sex you are."

"Ho, I can't see why that would interest you at all. Unless you wouldn't gain such perverse pleasure trying to embarrass a man?"

I grinned wider.

"Incorrigible man!"

"I like to see your reaction. It's never what I imagine

it will be," I admitted.

"You know, when I took this job on as a favour to Karen, I never thought I would have to endure daily torments from a grouchy trick playing rogue."

"Ah, it's good to see you appreciate my efforts."

"Now that's a change."

"What?" I asked with a twinkle in my eye as she smothered my face with moisturiser and dropped a towel in my lap

"A smug looking dragon," she said.

"What? You're calling me a dragon now? I thought I was Mr Rochester?"

"You're both. They seem to go hand in hand to me, and perfectly describe you. Although, I might have to add an imp to the mix."

I chuckled. "You must like the combination, since we get on so well."

"I'm a victim of circumstance. Out of sense of duty to my friend, I've put up with your mischievous ways."

"Come now Jane, you enjoy it really. Don't I brighten your day as much as your colourful outfits do mine?"

"Your face is done. Can you stand up, so I can get you painted?"

I stood up and faced the door. "My back first?" I asked as I craned my head over my shoulder. "Are you checking out my arse?"

She jumped and gave a little titter. "It's hard not to, buns of steel. Have you had implants?"

"Most certainly not. I'm one hundred percent natural."

"Not one hundred percent. I'm sure you weren't born with a woolly over your love wand. Are you leaving it on?"

"Do you want me to take it off?" I asked, raising an eyebrow as I looked over my shoulder.

"Ugh, not really. Isn't there a modesty pouch or a G-string you can wear instead? What are you chuckling about?"

"Only you would call a penis a love wand, and I have a Hibue to cover my unmentionables."

"Glad to hear it. Do you need some help to put it on?"

"Only at the back. The rest I can manage on my own."

The door to my dressing room opened, and Jane gasped as she shrunk behind my back.

"What the fuck are you wearing!" Alisha screeched. "I came here to talk to you while you were sober and here you are with little Miss Mouse playing sex games!"

Jane stepped out from behind my back and straightened her shoulders. "I resent the insinuation that there is something untoward going on between Mr Austin and myself."

I opened my mouth, about to intercede when Alisha waved a finger in my face and then pointed to my sock.

"If it's all innocent, what the hell is that?"

"It's a sock, and it's acting as a modesty pouch. Mr Austin's Hibue has been misplaced and until we can find another one to match his skin tone, we made a compromise. I'm sure you wouldn't want him to stand here naked?"

Alisha narrowed her eyes.

"You don't honestly believe he would be even the tiniest bit interested in me, do you?" She continued. "Even I can see the striking differences in attractiveness between you and myself. Why would he choose me over you? Wouldn't you agree it's ludicrous?"

"Laughable, yes." Alisha agreed as she turned to me. "But darling, you've been acting so odd lately. Not like you normally would at all. What's a girl supposed to think?"

Before I could make a comment, her mouth was on mine. Jane forgotten. Her bright clothing blending in with the monochrome wallpaper as though she was never there. I prised Alisha off me and guided her gently to the door.

"I'm really busy at the moment. I have to be on set in a matter of minutes, but I promise we'll talk later as soon as I'm finished."

She pouted her lips. "You'll take me out to dinner? Somewhere special to make up for everything?"

I opened the dressing room door, careful to keep most of myself covered and gnawed on my lip. How was I going to get out of this without causing a scene? There were already a few people hovering around with their phones at the ready. I gritted my teeth and pecked her on the cheek. "Sure, wherever you want to go. You book it and I'll be there. Just text me, okay?"

Alisha walked off, smiling.

"Can't a guy get his body paint on without an

audience?" I asked.

The crowd dispersed as I closed the door and looked over at Jane.

"I'm so sorry about that, Jane. You needn't have defended me. It was me who was to blame." I ran my hand through my hair. "I wish you hadn't said those things about yourself."

Jane crept out of the shadows. "I only spoke the truth. It is ridiculous to think anything would go on between you and me."

Eve opened the dressing room door. "They need you on set. Shit, you haven't even got your body paint on."

"Sorry, give us a minute and he'll be ready," Jane said.

"It wasn't her fault. Alisha threw a spanner in the works."

"A spanner? Is that what you call what you're wearing?" She lifted an eyebrow, then directed her gaze at Jane. "Ten minutes."

CHAPTER 10

BETH

Later that day, as I took off Tom's makeup for the last time. I wished that we could have a moment alone, so I could say goodbye properly. But everyone buzzed around him like bees to a jam pot and as soon as he was free of makeup, he had to rush off to make the date at the restaurant with Alisha. I didn't think anyone had mentioned to him it was my last day. Not that I expected anything from him, but good luck wishes. After all, I was the substitute, the stand in, nothing more.

I hopped from foot to foot as Tom strode away from me, heading for the exit. It seemed wrong to just walk away without at least telling him I wouldn't see him again. Even though his talk of friendship had probably meant nothing at all, it still felt to me as though I was leaving a beloved pet at an animal sanctuary while it was sleeping, and when it awoke, it would look around and find no one familiar.

"Tom," I called. My voice came out high, unnatural, hardly sounding like mine at all.

He looked over his shoulder. "Sorry Jane, I've got to run. This is something I must do. Speak to you later?" He turned back to the door and held up his hand in farewell.

I nodded, watching the door close, and my heart gave a jolt. Eve walked up to me, taking hold of my shoulder and asked. "Can you give me a minute before you leave?"

"Yes, of course," I replied, picking up my things. "Are you free now? I'm all done."

"Yes, we'll use Tom's dressing room as an office."

She opened the door and made her way to the makeup chair, took a seat, and gestured to the spare chair. "I'll cut to the chase. When you first came in to cover Karen, I was sceptical. I thought a girl who worked at a beauty parlour wouldn't be able to cut it on set, but you surprised me. Tom's makeup has been flawless, and you've even built a rapport with him. Which isn't always an easy thing. I'm not saying Mr Austin is difficult, but he doesn't take fools lightly and he expects the same amount of dedication as he himself gives to the craft."

"We get on well," I agreed.

"Yes, well, that's not so important now. Another few weeks and the Ironclaw set will close until next season. However, Karen told me you had handed in your notice at the Beauty Parlour. That you found you enjoyed working on set and fancied a change, is that right?"

"Yes, I've enjoyed the challenge of something new."

"Well, I have a proposition for you. There's an opening in London's fashion week. It will get you a foot in the door to work with some of the best in the industry. You'll get to meet some famous photographers, and if you work hard and show them what you can do, who knows where that will take you? And then, in a couple of months, if you're free, I would like you to come back and work for me, one of my staff's leaving to have a baby, and I'd like you to take up her position. What do you say?"

My mouth dropped open. "I... I, that sounds amazing. Would I just be covering maternity leave, or would it be permanent?" The thought of a pair of smiling blue eyes dusted with amber and brown popped into my mind, and my heart thumped wildly in my chest. Never mind about dreaming of seeing Mr Rochester again, I told myself. This is an opportunity of a lifetime.

"Nothing's permanent in this industry, Beth. But no, they don't intend to come back."

"I loved working on set. And the chance to work on Ironclaw or one of the other productions would be a dream come true."

"That's great. Here's Lawrence's number. Give him a ring and he'll arrange for you to go in and make up one of their models. Livy's going on her maternity leave on the 29th of April, if you contact me a fortnight before we can synchronise our schedules. If you're not free, I'll have enough time to replace you."

"Oh, I'll be available. I'd kill for this job." I laughed, trying not to snort. "Well, not literally!"

I left the set with a jaunty step. The thought of returning to my growly, gorgeous trickster made my feet feel as though they were gliding on ice, perfectly balanced with friction as a thing of the past. I knew it was illogical to have a high from this tenuous connection to Tom, and that he would forget me as quickly as leaves falling in the harshest of winters, but I couldn't help it – a fire burned within me when I thought of him.

When I returned to the apartment I shared with two friends - one my best friend Susie and the other, my self-declared bestie, Hunter Brando - I went straight over to my dressing table and took a notelet out of the drawer. Looking at it with a critical eye, I wondered if Tom would mind receiving a letter with, "Congratulations, it's a baby boy!", and a cute blue bunny plastered over the top of it? Since it was the only one I had, I thought it would be better than nothing and might even raise a smile from the indomitable Mr Rochester's side of his personality.

After an hour of pen chewing and crossing out, I picked up the battlefield-stained notelet and slipped it into its envelope, and then grimaced when I noticed the exterior looked as though the crime scene department had been dusting it for prints. I tapped out a message to Karen, asking if she could give the note to Tom for me.

I sighed, glared at the dirty smudges on my phone, and went to the bathroom to wash my hands. As I came out, Hunter opened the front door. Hunter was six foot two, muscle bound and almost as good looking as Tom. He was also a makeup artist and weekend drag queen at the Trap Door, a gay club in the heart of Soho. Everything about him screamed masculine perfection, apart from his eyebrows being a little too plucked and his voice crossed between Danny LaRue and, well, if I was being honest, David Beckham's. We often pulled his leg that his mother had hoped for a straight, kickboxing He-Man, who would bear her a brood of grandkids. And he always retorted with, "Pleaaase. If my mother had kept her legs closed any day of the week, she might have had a chance of knowing who my father was! And the last thing she wanted was a child to ruin her tantric yoga classes."

Contrary to common belief, Hunter's mother was, he has assured me many times, not a lady of the night, but a bored housewife, married to an equally work obsessed managing director of a vacuum parts manufacturing company. Oddly enough, the rest of the family were in medicine.

"Darling!" He air kissed me and pouted. "Are you all sad now you haven't got the man hunk to fondle every day?" He narrowed his eyes at my expression. "Oh, I was expecting tears. If not tears, at least a general fog of depression. What's happened? Jobless and man less should make even *you* a little downcast."

"Well, I'm sorry to disappoint you, but I don't think I am jobless. Well, I hope not. I've got an interview with Lawrence Day for London's fashion week."

"Shut the front door! What did you do, threaten someone? Maybe T A after all those tricks he played on you? You little cow, I've been trying to get a foot in there for years!"

"No, it was Eve. Tom had nothing to do with it. He didn't even know it was my last day." I frowned. "Although today's jest was a classic."

"Tell me more, girlfriend," he said, dragging me to the sofa.

We plonked ourselves down and I slid towards Hunter's body with alarming speed. I grabbed his thigh to stop myself from ending up on his lap.

"Hands off, babe. I know you struggle to keep your

fingers off this gorgeous piece of merchandise, but, sister, you'll just have to control yourself."

I giggled. "Yours is a poor second after what I've been dealing with today."

"No way! You never got to lay your eager little paws on Ironclaw's rippling muscles?"

I nodded. "He stripped down to a penis sock."

He frowned. "Tom Austin was wearing a penis sock? Why?"

"He thought it would be funny and hoped it would embarrass me enough that I'd do something stupid."

"Like take a picture? Please tell me you took a picture?" Hunter put his hands together and stared up at me with big puppy dog eyes.

"No, of course I didn't. I'm a professional." I rolled my eyes at him.

"Ah, Beth, you forgot your name. didn't you hun?"

"I forgot everything. Even how to breathe in and out and I swear my hands took a good five minutes massaging his arse."

"At least you had the excuse you were applying body paint."

I gave him a pained look.

He laughed. "You forgot that too!"

"Oh God, and then his beautiful girlfriend walked in and accused him of playing around with me. Can you believe it? And I've just written him a note to tell him I was sorry I left without saying goodbye. What an idiot I am. I bet he's glad to get rid of me!"

"Well, naturally. I would be."

My face crumpled.

"Oh, don't look at me like that! It was a joke! I said I would be, not that he was. I think the bloke has taken a shine to you." He gave me a nudge. "God knows why dressed like that! He probably has a thing for the homeless and bedraggled kittens. Are you going to lose the fancy dress and hat now you don't have to hide away from him anymore?"

I shrugged my shoulders.

"Ah, send him the note. What harm could it do? It's not as if you'll ever see him again."

"Well, I might. Eve says she wants me back when one of her staff goes on maternity leave." I turned to face him.

"Bloody hell, you must be a better makeup artist than I thought. 'Course you'd never know looking at you!"

"Meow," I replied.

"Darling, I don't know what's happened to you in the last month. Didn't you know you're supposed to make yourself more attractive when you fancy someone, not do an impression of a mad bag lady?"

"Hunter," I whined. "He'd never look at me like that in a million years. Have you seen his past girlfriends?"

"No, sweetie, I'm not interested in what they look like unless they're wearing Gucci. Although that picture of him emerging out of that hot tub is a different story. Are you sure he's straight?"

My eyes popped open. "You think he's gay?"

"Sadly, no I don't. A guy can but dream."

I scrolled through my phone and showed him pictures of all Tom's exes. Every one of them could enter a crowded room and make men adjust their trousers while their partners sneered their lips green with envy.

"Look at them Hunter. It's as though they were created in a factory. I bet they've never had a blemish. They must create a stir wherever they go looking that good."

"Dressed like that, I bet you have people staring open-mouthed whenever you enter a room!" Hunter chuckled.

I slapped his arm. "Harsh."

"You do it to yourself! Look honey, if you want to attract a guy, you can't hide your assets under a circus tent." He peered closer at the images. "Wow, I love that orange satin with puff sleeves and sexy side slit. It's fabulous!"

"That's Alisha, his current girlfriend. I'm sure you could borrow it if you asked. And why would I engage in such a fruitless activity? It's better for Tom and me to just be friends."

"Who wants *just* be friends with him?"

I pointed at my chest.

Hunter shook his head. "There's nothing wrong with setting your sights high. Anyhow, he isn't necessarily a catch. Looks aren't everything, and I bet he has a heap of bad habits. Okay, looking like that, you could forgive the nose picking and biting his fingernails in bed. And you never know whether he's into kooky girls."

"Thanks."

"Seriously, take the bull by the horns and send your precious letter. Stick your mobile number or address on the back. He might even look you up."

"Doesn't that smack of desperation?" I asked.

"No more than sending a Hollywood A-lister an apology for not saying goodbye when you filled in for his regular makeup artist, honey."

I groaned. "I was going to give it to Karen, but after what you've said, it seems silly."

He pulled me off the sofa. "Send your letter. Wasn't it he who went to the pub to find you?"

My brow creased, and I chewed on my lip. I picked my letter to him off the side and then put it down again.

"Sleep on it, darling. How about we order a pizza, and you make up my face and show me how talented you are?"

"What, you'll let me full drag you?"

Hunter did his own makeup, and he always looked fantastic.

"Tonight, you can have you wanton way with me, darling! If I don't like it, I'll scrub it off."

I squealed and clapped my hands as I followed him into his room. "You have no idea how long I've wanted to do this!"

He looked over his shoulder. "Ever since you found

out I was a drag queen," he replied drily.

CHAPTER 11

TOM

My mind flitted back to when Jane removed my makeup. Her continuous lip chewing and the way her fingers flitted over my face made me want to swot everyone away and asked her what the matter was. Had my nakedness freaked her out, or was it Alisha walking in and accusing us of fooling around that made her so skittish?

Of course, we were fooling around, but not in the way Alisha thought. Jane was a friend. A friend who was as dear to me as a favourite book: where you devour the pages ferociously, eager to finish but in the same breath, are desperate for it to last forever. The cover, all but forgotten, smudged and dogeared by constant handling.

My plain Jane, left like a brightly coloured toy out in the cold while her boy goes to warm himself by the fire. But I haven't forgotten her. Whatever was troubling her, I'd speak to her tomorrow. And maybe she'll make fun of me - how I've grown as a person when I tell her I've finished with Alisha because the physical attraction was no longer enough. Or perhaps she won't care? Although I chased that notion away as soon as it popped into my head, Jane would champion any cause I cared to follow.

As I exited the cab and pushed on the restaurant

door, I pulled on my jacket and straightened my shoulders. Perhaps this wasn't the best place to tell Alisha it was all over? Even though the maître d' was the only person who showed any interest when I walked in, and the place was swarming with celebrities and Russian oligarchs, I was sure word would get out in the press if Alisha caused a scene.

"Mr Austin, it's a pleasure to have you here tonight. Your companion has already taken her seat. If you'd like to follow me through, I'll show you to your table."

"Thank you."

"I don't believe we have had the pleasure before. My name is Franco. Charles is your server tonight. Any special dietary needs or requests, please let him know and he'll be able to make that happen for you. I hope you have a very enjoyable evening."

He led me over to where Alisha sat as a young man with wispy blonde hair and impeccable white shirt and black trousers pulled out a chair.

"Is this table to your liking, sir?" Charles asked.

I nodded. "Yes, thank you."

"Are there any special requests you have for tonight's dinner?"

"No, just the menu and a large bottle of still mineral water, please."

The man nodded and left. I leaned over the table and kissed Alisha on the cheek.

"Have you been here long?" I asked.

"No, only a few minutes. Isn't it fabulous? It was

so good of you to treat me like this and my favourite restaurant, too."

"Ah hem, yes."

What could I say? I hadn't the foggiest it was her favourite restaurant. I had heard of it, knew it was expensive, hard to book, and she only got a table because of my name. But the fact she used my fame to get it, only made me grit my teeth. This is what she wanted from me all along, a way of opening exclusive doors. I had the urge to get up and go, leave her there sitting like a fool, but contrary to common belief, not all publicity is good. When it's bad, it's bad, and I had worked too hard to ruin it over something like this.

Plus, my agent would never let me hear the end of it. He guarded my public face better than he did his crown jewels.

"You smile and keep me happy, and I will never mention I found you in your dressing room only wearing a sock with that gaudy little mouse," Alisha said with a smile on her face.

It took me a moment to realise she had just blackmailed me. "Bitch," I snarled under my breath.

"I said smile, Tom. You're an actor, I'm sure even one of your skill set can manage that?"

"What's the point to this, Alisha? You and I are over. Why would you want to pretend we're a couple when it isn't true?"

"I'm not bothered whether we're lovers. You weren't that great anyhow. But I want the life you lead. I want the parties, the fine restaurants, the red carpets."

"I'm not even a big party person," I said, flapping a napkin over my lap.

"I'm sure you can manage it with the right motivation. Think of it as a role. Be convincing without hiding behind that pretty face or Ironclaw's fancy makeup."

"Are you sure you're up to role playing? After all, you're an actress and even with your stunning looks, your career hasn't taken off. Perhaps you're not as fine an actress as you think you are?"

"It's much harder for a woman than a man. You do not know how sexist the film industry is."

"So, you're willing to ride on my coattails?"

"It's better than some fumble with a dirty old man on a casting couch," she retorted.

I excused myself and went to the bathroom. Leaning on the sink, I gave my reflection a long, hard look. Although I could see her point, there was no way I'd let her blackmail me into this, damned what my agent thought. Tonight, however, I would give her a victory, a short one. I could weather the storm, but Jane, what would it do to her – to her career? How could I protect her from the insinuations that would follow? Everyone would insist there was no smoke without fire, even though our relationship was purely platonic. Would she lose her job because they would assume that she took advantage of her position, or would they make a laughingstock of her because she was unique and quirky and would never grace the cover of a glamour magazine?

Damn it, damn Alisha to hell!

My only option would be to speak to Rick, my agent, in the morning and then the studio and see if they could move Jane away from me until the noise settled down. Why couldn't one of my exes be more like Jane – fun, caring, interesting, brighten my day with their smile?

If only I fancied her, that would solve the Alisha situation perfectly.

I could pretend I fancied her? I'm an actor for god's sake, and a lot better than that bitch in there had suggested. It wouldn't take much for me to convince the tabloids and the public in general that I had gone for more than looks. It wouldn't be hard to have fun when we went out together. We already had a connection, just not a romantic one.

Exiting the gents, I plastered a smile on my face and went off to play the adoring lover. As I sat down, I noticed for the first time Alisha had a tiny wisp of grey by her ear and that when she wasn't smiling, her lips turned down. It gave me a sudden snapshot of what she'd look like in twenty years' time. Focusing on her mouth, I pictured a sneer and a look of dissatisfaction. Then Jane's smile flashed into my mind and my heart leapt against my ribs. I frowned. I didn't find Jane attractive, but her smile… well, you just had to reciprocate it and the way one side formed into a little dimple – too cute.

"I know you don't like my proposition, but I really thought you'd make more effort than this. Scowling away won't change anything and look on the bright side, you dating me won't harm your reputation one bit," Alisha said.

"Was I scowling? How is that possible when I'm

having such a delightful evening?" I wiped my mouth and threw the napkin on the table, and pushed my chair back.

"Oh, don't be so childish, Tom. You may even enjoy mixing, instead of skulking around with that mutt of yours and playing video games."

"It's not just a video game, it's a strategy adventure game and Drago isn't a mutt."

At that moment, Charles came over and pulled Alisha's chair out.

"Leaving so soon? I hope everything was to your liking?" he asked.

"It was wonderful. We'll come again next week." Alisha said, smiling and throwing me a warning look.

"That's good to hear." He turned to me. "Mr Austin?"

"Er, yes..." I wracked my brain, trying to remember what I'd eaten. "Excellent – if you like your balls crushed in a vise," I muttered.

"I beg your pardon, sir?"

"I said, very nice."

We headed out of the restaurant, and I hailed a cab.

"There's no need to invite me home, Tom."

"I wasn't going to. I'm not that desperate to get you in my bed, either."

"Oh, come on, Tom. You could never turn me down. You may think you're a better actor than me, but you're not a better lover."

"How do you know? Have you had a lot of clients vying for your charms?"

She slapped my face. Made it look playful, but it was harder than it looked. "I hope you aren't always going to behave so bitterly." A cab pulled up, and she got in. "I'll text you when I need your services again."

CHAPTER 12

BETH

"Oh, my god! You've made me even more gorgeous than normal! Who would have thought that was possible? Why haven't I let you do this before?" Hunter asked.

"Because you've never seen my work before," I replied.

"If you're capable of this, girlfriend, why don't you work some of the magic on yourself?" He circled his face with one purple crystal infused fingernail.

"I don't go out much to dress up."

"Fuck that! You can make me up whenever you want. Even if I'm just going to the chippy to pick up a battered sausage!"

I quirked my eyebrow. "Your definition of a battered sausage and mine vary wildly."

"Cheeky cow. Although, fairs fair, you're right. I can't help being so desirable I have every dog barking up this tree." His hands glided down his tight frame, and I could only nod in agreement. I wondered what Tom would look like in drag? Awful, I thought. There was nothing about his face that said female. Some men were androgynously handsome; Hunter, a prime example of it, but not Tom.

Made up, he'd look like a pantomime dame. "What are you thinking about?"

"Nothing, why?" I asked.

"Your lip did that weird Mona Lisa smile thing, and your dimple appeared."

"I don't smile like the Mona Lisa!"

"Okay, I'll agree you don't, if you tell me what that weird da Vinci smile was for."

I grinned. "I was just picturing Tom in drag." I laughed harder as I took in his expression. "I know what you mean." I pulled a face, hoping I looked like the famous painting. "You did it too!"

"I did not!"

I nodded. "Yep, it's hard not to. It's like seeing fresh blooms on a steel girder."

His mouth twisted. "Yes, you're right, it's wrong with a capital R."

I screwed up my face. "Wrong with a capital R, you buffoon?"

"Yes, really 'rong."

We burst out in peals of laughter. Hugging each other for support.

"Hey guys, what have you been up to? What's so funny?" Susie asked as she opened the bedroom door.

Hunter and I jumped, which only made us giggle more. "'Rong," Hunter said.

"Definitely, 'rong," I agreed.

"What are you two clowns going on about? What's 'rong?"

"'Rong is 'rong," I smirked.

"'Rong is 'rong because it's not wight. Wight would be right if it wasn't wrong. Simple!"

"Have you been drinking?" Susie asked.

As we calmed down and stopped laughing at our silly joke, we followed her into the kitchen-cum-lounge.

Taking a deep breath, I asked, "When did the pizza come?"

"It arrived at the same time as I did."

"We'd better tuck in then. Beth, grab the plates," Hunter said.

"Are we sitting at the table? The sofa's behaving like a waterbed."

"Yes, me and Beth nearly got better acquainted than we wished to. She may even be having my baby!" He smirked. "Well, more than I wished to, who wouldn't want my baby? Still, when she gets her new job, perhaps we can club together and get a new one."

"You've got a new job?" Susie asked.

"Well, I've got an interview." I grinned and rolled my eyes at Hunter.

"That's great. Come and sit down and tell me all about it."

We carried the pizza box over to the table and sat down. "Hey, where did you put my letter, Sues?"

"Letter? Oh, was it the wrong one? Karen said you'd

asked her to pick one up?" She frowned. "I'm sure it was addressed to Tom. There wasn't another one, was there?"

"Oh, Mother!" Hunter piped up.

"What am I missing? Why are you so pale, Beth?"

"The cowardly custard hadn't decided whether to send it or not," Hunter said.

I bit my lip.

"Well, too late now, darling. The fate fairy has intervened. You know you would have sent it eventually."

"Yes, but I was going to change the paper," I said, crunching up my face at the thought of Tom opening my letter.

"Ah, I'm sure he'll love the butchered bunnies."

I grimaced. Susie took in my expression and remarked to Hunter, "You look gorgeous tonight. Did Beth do your face?"

Hunter grunted. "It appears everyone but me knew how talented she was. Why didn't anyone tell me? I could have taken the club by storm instead of going around like some sad faced Grayson Perry."

I'd just taken a sip of drink and cola spurted out of my nose as I tried not to spray it from my mouth.

Hunter guarded the pizza ineffectively with his bejewelled fingernails. But luckily, I had the good sense to turn my head away and cover the window with a fine spray of deep amber droplets.

"Gross," Hunter commented.

"It was your fault for coming out with such a

statement!" I said, wiping my chin with a tissue and mopping the glass. "Don't worry, I'll get the window cleaner out after we've eaten."

Hunter sneered his nose up.

Susie grinned. "It could have been worse. Beth might have been eating pizza, and then the window would look as though the leftovers from a zombie's dinner were splattered up the glass."

Hunter covered his mouth and faked retched into his hand as I giggled. "You didn't have to suggest that, Susie." Hunter glared, which only made Susie laugh.

CHAPTER 13

TOM

After a few hours wrestling with my covers, I untangled my legs from the sheets and sat up in bed. The linen pooled in my lap, tenting over my crotch. I looked down at the bulge and frowned. Why was everyone behaving oddly?

Alisha blackmailing me wasn't the cause of my condition. I was sure of that. I hadn't been thinking of her. I had been thinking of taking Jane out as a ruse to get the bitch off both our backs. So, why did I have an erection? I didn't like Jane in that way. Okay, every time she laid her hands on me, something stirred within. Alright, not only within, but that was normal, right? Because every time I had a body paint, I became hard. Not. I screwed my eyes up.

Then there was the look on Jane's face yesterday. What was bothering her? Or was it only me making something out of nothing, because I wanted her to confide in me, to open up like a clam and reveal the inner pearl. Perhaps no one was acting odd other than me?

Blackmail wasn't a startling development from Alisha. I knew she had a ruthless, manipulative gold-digging streak, but I bypassed all that because she was beautiful, and I wanted her in my bed. And now, I'm sitting with a stonker of a hard-on thinking about someone I don't fancy. Not even remotely!

If Jane's hand trailed down my chest now, I wouldn't feel a thing. Hell! I kicked the covers off and headed for the shower. Drago raised his head and whined as I shot past him.

"No, I need a shower," I told him, running past. He gave me a look as if he found my predicament hilarious and rolled over on his back with his feet in the air.

As I came back into the bedroom, a towel wrapped around my waist, I wondered if I had some strange predilection. Perhaps the mystery of not really knowing Jane's real name and the way she looked turned me on? Yes, it was me acting odd. I reached a hand up to my forehead. Was I hot? Maybe there was a virus going around?

"I could be falling for something," I said out loud. Drago groaned and flopped on his side. "Don't you think I could be falling for something, boy?"

He groaned again and laid a paw over one eye.

"You're no flaming help at all!" I growled.

He got up, shook himself and nudged open my bedroom door. Seconds later, he returned with his lead in his mouth.

"Okay, you win. I'll take you for a walk."

***

Before I arrived at the set, I'd made a quick call to Rick. He was in the middle of something and agreed to ring me back. It was unlike him to brush me off. I was his number one client, and we had formed a friendship over the years, which had both of us scratching our heads as to why. On the face of it, we had nothing in common, apart from a mutual interest in my career and Universal War Warriors, an online game we loved to play.

Then I walked into my dressing room. I stood at the door, my mouth agape. Karen hovered by my dressing table, engrossed in a heated phone conversation.

"You prick!" she stormed. "You promised me that this would be our time, but two days away and you're back to the same old excuses. Well, don't bother calling me again. I've wasted enough of my life waiting for you, and honey, you just aren't worth the agro!"

She hung up and turned to face me. "Oh, hello darling! Did you miss me?"

"Karen, you're back?" I said, trying to iron the crease from my brow.

"Yes, didn't you know?" She gave a little shrug.

"I knew you were back home, but where's your friend?" I entered the room and closed the door. The bottom of my stomach dropped, and I frowned in confusion. Why did seeing Karen leave me with a hole in my chest?

"Well, this isn't the response I thought I'd get from you! Haven't you missed me at all?" She burst into tears. I strode forward and wrapped an arm around her shoulder.

"Of course I did." I lied. I bit my tongue, itching to ask what had happened to Jane, but knowing this wasn't the time. "What happened in Monaco?"

She wiped the tears from her face. "Monaco was wonderful. It's only since I've got back everything has turned to shit."

"Why, what's happened?" I feigned interest.

"He said he'd be over next month, but now he's making excuses. Saying he has to go back to Hollywood and direct a new movie."

I bit my lip. Guy Fawkes. I knew this because I was the lead, but I didn't want to get involved with their lover's quarrel. If Toby kept things from Karen, who was I to put her straight? I didn't think he did it to hurt her, he just had a busy life, and he couldn't say no to opportunities when they arrived. The man was a brilliant director, but a lousy partner.

"Why not travel out there and meet him? You have connections in the trade. Why not use them to find work out there?" Shut up, man. I thought as I gnawed my lip. My tongue swiped at the metallic tang invading my mouth.

"Oh, you're travelling out there after Ironclaw finishes. You could put a word in for me, couldn't you, darling?"

"Er, well, you know I don't have a say on that side of things, don't you?"

"But you're a big star. They'd take notice of what you say."

I grimaced. The door opened and Eve popped her

head in.

"Karen, good to see you back. Now you've settled in, can you get on with your job? Tom's needed on set."

"Yes, right on it, darling. We were just catching up."

"Catching up on what? Never mind, Karen, just get the job done. I've had enough drama this morning without you adding to it."

Karen silently got on with my makeup, her face like thunder. Her fingers pressed into my skin as though they were hailstones on glass. I stared at a rainbow-coloured brush on the counter. She must have left it behind, I thought. Is that what made her call me back yesterday? Was she fidgety because she wanted to say goodbye?

Eventually, I had to say something. I couldn't stand the suspense. "What's happened to Jane?" I growled.

Karen's face turned from black to grey. As blank as a winter's day. "Jane?"

"Your friend. The one that filled in for you." I tapped my fingers on the arm of the chair. "The one who was at the pub."

Her eyes narrowed. "Why do you want to know?"

My mouth tightened. Was she trying to be obtuse? "We became friends, and I wondered what had happened to her."

"Friends? You think you and she are friends? Since you're such good friends, you'll have her phone number, and you can find out for yourself."

"Why the sarcasm, Karen? I only wanted to know if she was alright." I picked up the brush. "This is hers. I thought I could drop it in for her at sometime."

She snatched it out of my fingers. "No need, I can return it. I called in last night, but she was too busy to see me, giggling away with some bloke in the other room. I thought it prudent not to disturb them."

A muscle in my jaw ticked and as Karen turned to the mirror, her lips turned up. Was it true? Karen looked extremely smug all of a sudden. Then why would she lie? They were friends. A friend wouldn't sabotage… what? Another friendship? A male showing an interest? Was that what I was? I ground my teeth together and glared at my reflection in the mirror. I wasn't sure whose image I was trying to erase with my x-ray vision. It was quite possible I wouldn't be happy until the whole mirror became a dazzling pile of fine sand.

On the plus side, Alisha wouldn't have any fire without kindling. I could make sure no one gave her name away from the studio and Jane would disappear back into obscurity as though she were a magical sprite. I wished she was a magical sprite, so she could pop in and out of my life whenever I needed her. Stroke her fingers across my face and charge the battery within with her electric touch. But that was a fantasy and the only one I pursued with any relish was chilling in front of the telly when I played War Warriors.

As the day progressed, I found myself counting the hours until it was time to go home. It was something I hadn't done for weeks, ever since the breath of fresh air that was Jane came into my life. How one person could make such a difference to the simplest thing was something I never thought I'd comprehend. Coffee tasted richer, hours turned to minutes, punches into taps. What else but a sprite could accomplish all this?

Had I missed Karen after six weeks? No. But I missed Jane, almost the moment I stepped out of the set door the night before.

I glanced at my phone and noticed there was a new message. For a moment, my heart raced in my chest. Did Jane have my number? My hand trembled as I pressed my thumb to the sensor and tapped on the envelope.

'Be ready in half an hour. You're taking me to the movies. A'

I groaned and gritted my teeth. Flipped the screen to Rick's number and placed the call.

"Why haven't you rung me back?" I asked.

"Tom? Had a great day, have you?"

"Do I sound as if I've had a great day?" I pushed open the set door and let in bang against the wall.

"Eh, I was just about to ring you back."

I stood still, waiting for him to come up with an excuse. "Now? You haven't tried to before?"

"Thomas, you know I have your best interest at heart. I heard through the grapevine that the source of this trouble has left. That leaves only her word against yours."

"How did you hear that, Richard?" I snarled, tempted to call him Dick to really wind him up.

He voice held a smugness to it. "I have connections."

I could picture him tapping his nose as though he had the answer to everything. "These connections, do they go as far as telling you where the source of the problem went? And did these 'connections' of yours tell you that Eve was also a witness to the sock scandal?"

"Well, no, but that's hardly important, is it? And Eve won't say anything."

"It's important to me. And, Rick, you might have been my agent for years, but if you ever leave me hanging like you have today..." I disconnected the call and put the phone on silence.

By the time a car came to pick me up to take Alisha and me to the movies, I had thirty missed calls.

***

"So, what little treat have you got planned tonight?" I asked drily as I got into the car.

"Now, Tom, I told you to bring your happy face with you," said Alisha.

"This is my happy face. Haven't you noticed? I always look this way when I'm with you?"

Looking over at me, she sneered. "I believe you're right! You only looked ecstatic when you were about to come." She pulled a face, which, I supposed, was a mimic of my come face.

"I think it goes more like this." I screwed up my eyes and let my tongue stick out. A goofy smile stretching my lips wide.

She laughed. "Wow, mean and moody tonight. Just remember as soon as we get out of the car, I want you to play the adoring boyfriend."

"And if I don't?"

"You know what will happen if you don't. You, your sock and little Miss mouse will be plastered all over the tabloids."

"This sock?" I asked, pointing to my ankle, where I wore a traditional man's black sock.

"You're very facetious this evening, Tom. We both know what I'm referring to."

"Ah, we," I signal between us, "know what sock you mean, but would anyone else? Have you got photographic evidence?"

Her mouth twisted. "I don't need it. I only have to say the word and the rumour will spread like wildfire. And little Miss mouse will go scurrying back to her hole."

"What little Miss mouse are you referring to?" I asked.

"The plain primp princess." Alisha rolled her eyes.

"Do you mean Karen, my makeup artist?"

Fire flashed into her eyes. "No, I don't mean Karen. I meant that gaudy bitch you've taken a liking to!"

I nodded with a smile on my face, the first one since I entered the car.

"Where did you say we were going to?" I asked.

"The Electric Cinema on Portobello Road. Some hotshot friend of yours has hired the whole thing and is hosting a review of their latest movie."

"Which friend?" I frowned. "And how come you

know about it, but I don't?"

"Tally Califf. And they messaged me. They knew you wouldn't reply."

I nodded. Too right I wouldn't. I couldn't stand the pompous little git. At least they held it at the Electric, which meant I could get away with having a nap with any luck. The seats were enormous.

"Have we got a seat or a bed?" I asked.

"As I told you before, I have no interest in bedding you again."

"I was hoping for a nap. I can't say I'd be too keen to act out a love scene in the middle of the cinema."

"No, you're not that exciting a lover."

"Bah, I've never had complaints before."

"That's because you were asleep before you found out." she said, tossing her long brunette curls over her shoulder.

I lifted an eyebrow. "Now who's bitter?"

***

The film was better than I thought. Although I fell asleep during part of it. Tally had provided dinner and wine, which improved the film tenfold, and almost everyone I didn't want to speak to left me alone. I even had a very pleasant dream that I was a dog, and my owner, who looked unsurprisingly like Jane, stroked my coat until she got a rise out of me. When I awoke, I had to adjust my trousers and was more than a little tempted to visit the gents for a touch of R&R - romping and releasing. But after receiving a few raised eyebrows from those at the urinals as I entered the stalls, I thought better of it.

As we exited the cinema, my arm draped over Alisha's shoulder, a flash from the throng of reporter's' cameras greeted us.

"Your doing?" I asked from the corner of my mouth as I smiled into the lens.

"You don't think I'd do this for nothing, do you?"

"Most certainly not. Why have a cash cow if you don't milk it?" I held the door open to let her get in. I leant in and said, "Thanks for the evening. Don't call me. We won't be doing this again."

"What the hell do you mean?"

"Do your worst. I don't react well to blackmail." I slammed the door closed.

"You'll regret this." I saw her mouth.

I blew her a kissed and walked off. A trail of reporters followed me five blocks. Bombarded with a deluge of questions, I strolled the streets with a smile on my face and the only comment I made was. "Isn't it a beautiful night for a stroll?" In fact, it was like immersing myself in a plunge pool where ice had formed on the top, but I couldn't wipe the smile from my face however hard my teeth chattered.

CHAPTER 14

BETH

I was lucky enough to get the job for Lawrence Day at London fashion week, and for most of the spring I picked up contract work off the backs of photographers I'd met while working there. I also spent more time with Hunter, honing my skills of the more Avant Garde side of makeup, and became a regular at the Trap Door - a favourite with the girls as they vied for my attention.

"Beth, just look at my foundation, honey. Do I look like someone has tangoed me?" Cherise asked.

I laughed. "You've been what?"

"She's asking if she's too orange. Cherise, I don't know why you're worried now. You haven't fussed about looking like Donald Trump for the last five years!" Hunter replied.

"Bitch," Cherise replied.

"Hey Beth Darling, what do you think of these lashes? Do they make me de-sire-a-bul?"

"They make you look like an old cow, if that's what you were aiming for?" Hunter said, his voice dropping an octave.

For once, I saw the masculine side of Hunter. He guarded me as though I was the holy grail and if someone had given him a sword, I'm sure he would have run many of his friends through. But for all the grousing, I spent most of my free time at the club, primping the 'girls', swapping hair and makeup tips and talking about men. It was the perfect place to keep me busy and bury myself in a world where Tom Austin existed only as a male fantasy, which was exactly where he should be for a girl like me. Not someone I once shared a tenuous connection with. Someone who, for a few short weeks, I regarded as a friend – more than a friend. How much more, burst like a bubble when there was no response from my letter. I guess the butchered bunnies never made an impact on Tom, at least, not the right one.

And that was another odd thing. Karen had returned almost none of my texts. Her phone, when I rang always went through to voicemail and I'd only received a few short sharp messages in the last few months. It wasn't like her at all, which made me spend hours going over past conversations and analysing every word I'd spoken to her and every text I'd sent. Had I somehow upset her? I knew she'd been busy ever since her return to the Ironclaw set and as soon as that had dried up, she'd flown off to Hollywood and worked on the set of Guy Fawkes, Tom's latest movie.

I swallowed hard, losing two good friends, tugged my heart from my chest, and one in particular, crushed it on the pavement under their heel. The fact, it was the taller, broader of the two, made me berate myself for being such a fool.

"Stop standing there all misty-eyed, Beth." Hunter

said, giving me a nudge.

"What? I was not!" Makeup brush in hand, I flushed to my roots and considered wearing a hat again.

"Oh honey, it's as plain as day when you're thinking of sock man. Anytime one of the girls mentions his name, you go all static and cow-eyed."

"I wasn't thinking of him. I was thinking about Karen." I bit my lip.

"You're a terrible liar Beth. Never play poker and as for Karen's behaviour, it reeks of a guilty conscience or the green-eyed monster to me."

I frowned. "What? You think Karen is jealous, but why? It doesn't make any sense."

"No, neither was my urge to strangle you with my stockings the entire time you worked with Lawrence Day."

"You didn't!"

"You never felt that looming presence over your shoulder, then?"

I laughed. "Yeah, but you guys always loom over me, I'm practically a dwarf." I glanced over at Lola. "Sorry Lola, I meant a person of restricted height."

At 5 foot 1 I could never describe myself as tall, but at a foot taller than Lola, I was like a giant.

"You don't have to worry about being politically correct with me, hun. I'm short and sassy and proud of it, the only dynamic dwarf in this joint. Anyway, guys like it and you'll never hear me complain of having bad knees." Lola winked outrageously and sauntered off in three-inch heels.

"Sex bomb," Hunter said with a smirk. "And she's right, I've got no complaints."

My eyes popped wide open. "No, Hunter! You never!"

"Of course I did. It would have been rude to say no. Not quite the best, but definitely a close second. There was that grandpa without a tooth in..."

I clapped my hand over Hunter's mouth. "There are some things a friend should never know!" I drew an invisible zip along Hunter's mouth and threw away the key.

He shrugged but didn't say another word, on that subject at least. Although, in hindsight, I should have stayed on the subject of Hunter's best blow job ever.

"So, have you had a call from Eve yet?" he asked.

"No, perhaps she doesn't want me anymore. It's well past the time when the woman was going on maternity leave."

"Well, honey, if the worst comes to the worst and she doesn't call, at least you have plenty of work."

"Yes, there is that." I looked at my feet, trying to ignore the ache in my chest.

Hunter wrapped his arm around my shoulder and gave me a squeeze. "Look on the bright side, love. One day you'll see him again... in his next big movie or on the cover of some glossy magazine with his wife and three beautiful children."

"Thanks, a bundle. We all need friends like you, Hunter. Have you got a rope handy, or a silver gripped lady's pistol?" I asked, mimicking shooting myself in the head.

He laughed and shook his head.

"Bottle of pills, a capsule of arsenic?"

"No, but if you come out front and watch Tucum Under, it will do the job just as well."

***

Three days later, Eve called, all apologetic and begging me to forgive her and come in as soon as possible for a chat. I had a break in my day around noon and if I hopped on my bike and pedalled over to the studios, then I'd have an hour free to pick up lunch and discuss terms. With my heart pumping in my chest, I got on my bike and pedalled like crazy, swinging into the studios, my head down with my mind full of a deep laugh and blue eyes shot through with reflections of sunrise. And that's when it happened.

Some idiot, with too much money, opened the door to their swanky Range Rover without looking and catapulted me to the pavement. Dressed in Lycra, I looked as though I'd been involved in a gravel shredding crash on the tour de France. Blood poured from a cut on my knee and elbow. I groaned as a hand wrapped around my arm and dragged me to my feet.

"I'm so sorry. God, you were fast. I never saw you coming. Are you alright?"

I shook off the hand and stumbled to my feet, flushing to my roots as pain lanced through my limbs and concentrated on my bum. I glanced down to find much of my buttock on display; the flesh studded with meteors of stone in their bloody setting. Alright, maybe not meteors, but that's what it felt like to me. Especially when my attacker, cum rescuer, tried to brush said meteors from my arse.

"Hands off, thank you very much." I said, dabbing at the tears in my eyes.

"Are you alright?"

I glared at the man's face and faltered. Tom? I lowered my head.

His head dipped. "Do I know you from somewhere?" he asked.

"No," I mumbled. "Why would you think that? I'm a nobody."

He took off his jacket and attempted to cover my shoulders with it, while I tried to ignore the touch of his hands and shuck the garment off.

He frowned. "I'm only trying to help."

My stomach rolled, bubbling like a witch's cauldron. Why did it have to be him? He didn't want to know me. His offer of friendship was his way of being polite, nothing more, otherwise he would have answered my letter, and now he didn't even recognise me. I glanced at the ground. My buckled bicycle lay at my feet, a wheel sticking out at a jaunty angle like a dislocated joint.

We both bent to pick up the debris of my once sleek racer and crashed heads. Straightening, a gust of wind erupted from my behind as heat flashed into my face. Had he noticed? Involuntarily, I took in a deep breath, sniffed, stepped back, and prayed the opposite was true to the adage; silent but violent. As a precaution, I waved my hands about on the way down from rubbing my head.

"Jane, did you just blow a hole through your leggings?" he asked with a lopsided grin, while rubbing his own head.

I grabbed my bike and started limping away while trying to hide my backside, just in case that was exactly what had happened. My humiliation complete, I dragged it to the other side of the Range Rover.

"No," I replied, "to both counts. I don't know what you're talking about!"

He strode over to me and grabbed me in a crushing embrace. My cycle helmet dropped over my eye, my tongue lolled out of my mouth and for a second, I closed my eyes and sunk into the familiar scent of Mr Rochester. But just as I was about to wrap my arms around him, he stood back, turned his back on me and stalked off.

"Bitch," he muttered.

My brow furrowed, and with my bike hanging from the handlebars by one hand, I dropped it to the pavement and walked away.

***

"Christ, what happened to you?" Eve gasped as I walked through the door.

"Bike, I don't know!" I burst into tears.

For the second time that day, arms encircled my shoulders and wrapped me in a warm embrace. At first, I stood rigid, frozen, letting the tears cascade down my face and bubbles blow out of my nose and then my shoulders sagged, and I dropped my snot infested face onto Eve's Herve Leger satin top.

"What happened Beth?"

I dried my tears on my tattered top and shook my head. "Mr Rochester knocked me off my bike and then hugged me."

She frowned. "Are you badly hurt?"

I bit my lip. "Yes, he called me a bitch."

"What?"

I shrugged my shoulders.

"I'll get you the first aid kit and a lovely cup of tea with plenty of sugar. You're in shock, and you'll need something to wear. I'll see what I can find."

Half an hour later, I exited the set with a new contract and hopped into the cab Eve had called for me. My taste buds were still pulsing from the overdose of sugar zinging in my mouth. I ran a tongue around my teeth and asked the driver to pull into a local newsagent for a bottle of water and some chewing gum. I received a few raised eyebrows as I walked through the shop and purchased my goods, but mostly everyone ignored me, (being in London, you never knew what you might see any day of the week), until a little boy pinched at my leg and said, "Hey you, I never knew Mordork's were ugly chicks."

I looked down into his chubby face and grubby

fingers and said, "I'll let you into a secret," I bent stiffly and whispered into his ear. "They can be whatever they want, boy or girl. One minute, they're buying gum from Mr Snappy Shopper, the next, they're slaying human scum who leave fingerprints on their uniforms." I pulled a face and watched him back off.

His mother took hold of his hand and tugged him to her. "Leave the weirdo alone, Heathcliff."

"Heathcliff," I sniggered.

The boy turned around and flipped me the bird as his mother dragged him from the shop.

"Nice." I left the shop and got back into the taxi.

"Haven't I met you before?" asked the cabby.

I looked at the reflection in the rear-view mirror and shrugged. "It's possible?"

"What are you doing dressed up like that this afternoon? I thought Ironclaw had finished filming."

"You're very well informed," I replied.

"I often do their pickups when they're filming there."

"Oh." I shrunk back in my seat.

"There was this really odd girl, who was a right nightmare I used to pick up. Apparently, she was a brilliant makeup artist, but jeez, you should have seen the state of her!"

I nodded politely as my insides turned to ice.

"I thought she had some highly contagious disease when I first took her to the set. Frightened the living crap out of me. What did you say you were doing this afternoon, love?"

I swallowed. "Fancy dress party?" I said.

It was a testament to the people I worked with that they never said a word about how I was dressed when I returned to the photographer's studio later that afternoon.

CHAPTER 15

TOM

The first time in months I'd seen Jane, and she fell at my feet. Okay, perhaps that's not an accurate description of what happened. But something bizarre occurring was one hundred percent natural for her. It was not natural for me to open my car door and have a damsel crashing to the pavement like a rag doll at my feet. A cute, slightly windy, with a firm butt, nice ankles, and liquid brown eyes. Damsel?

What the hell does 'damsel' mean, anyway? It sounds romantic and whimsical, a damsel in distress. The knight went to save the damsel from the fearsome dragon.

Odd?

Eight months ago, I would have described Alisha as a damsel. Strike that, a dame, a diva, a femme fatale. Never a damsel – a damsel suggested, to me, a type of innocence and charm, of naivety.

And Jane would have been what? A nobody – is that what she described herself as? An unearthed gem, because it's true, I would have passed her in the street without a second's thought, and yet, that was folly. Jane was worth uncovering.

And Alisha was like the wicked witch, turning up in the nick of time to weave her evil spell and tear the lovers apart. Lovers? Where did the lovers come into my relationship with Jane? Relationship?

Thinking like this was spinning me in circles. All I knew was that when I saw Jane again, my heart fluttered in my chest like a caged bird and all the annoyance of the day flew away. Until that bitch showed up, phone in hand, giving the evil eye, and my gaze turned red.

I stormed across the lot, screeching to a halt in front of Maleficent. Actually, Maleficent wasn't nearly as wicked.

"What are you doing here?" I demanded.

"I have just as much right to be here as you, Tom. After all, I am an actress." She took a step nearer. "We used to be friends."

"That's something we never were."

"Lovers, then." She pouted.

"We had sex." I glanced over my shoulder, but Jane was nowhere in sight. "Just keep out of my business, Alisha." I turned on my heel and walked away. Even her bike was gone. Alisha said something to my back, but I wasn't listening.

***

The next morning, I awoke to Drago bringing me my morning paper. I groaned as I took in the front cover.

"Beauty fells the Beast." The news headline shouted. There was a picture of Jane at my feet, looking battered and torn. The way the photographer had captured the image made the handlebars look like horns sticking out of Jane's head. There was another picture with me hugging Jane to my chest, her hat askew, her tongue lolling out of her mouth, followed by the caption 'Beauty slays the Beast'. The item said, Hollywood A-lister had the misfortune of a fan falling at his feet, desperate for him to take notice of her. The unknown female, obviously a stranger to the beauty business, then collapsed against him, but heroic hunk Tom Austin bravely fought off the less than captivating creature's unwanted attention.

I gritted my teeth and threw the paper across the room. Drago gave me a look and went to sit in his basket.

"It wasn't you, boy, it was that she-devil. The vicious bitch sent off those pictures and probably suggested the headlines, too. Can you believe how they've made Jane look?" I strode back and forth across the floor. Drago tilted his head to one side and gave me a sympathetic look. "It's not me who needs your sympathy. It's Jane. geez, how do I put this right?"

Drago got out of his basket and paced with me.

"Think man, think." I muttered, running a hand through my hair. "Why was Jane at the studios?" Then it hit me. She was there about a job. She was heading toward DarkMatter Studios for an appointment with Eve Sharp. That had to be it! Eve was employing her for the new series of Ironclaw. My emotions soared and then dropped – Alisha and Jane working in the same place!

I had to set a plan in motion. First things first. Ring

Rick and put in a complaint into the papers. The studio had a privacy policy where no one could leak photos to the press. Since there was only one other person besides Jane and me, I could prove Alisha was the culprit and get her fired from whatever production she was working on. Then I had to source a new bike for Jane and find out her address from Eve. Perhaps even put a word in that I wanted her to be my head makeup artist? Karen was still in America, loving it up with Toby and I wasn't even sure whether she would come back. Although it wouldn't be unfortunate if she stayed out there.

"Eve, it's Tom. The makeup artist who filled in for Karen, can you give me her address?"

"The one you made cry when you knocked her off her bike and then called her a bitch?" she asked. I could just imagine her crossing her arms over her chest and jutting a hip out.

Silence fell as I wracked my brains about why Jane thought I'd called her a bitch, and then the penny dropped, with a clang.

"Eve, you don't understand. I didn't call her a bitch. It was Alisha, she was standing there with her phone…"

"So, it was Alisha who sent those pictures into the paper?"

I bit my lip. I wasn't a gossipmonger; I'd been in the public eye too long to spend my time spreading rumours. "Look Eve, I'm dealing with this. You never heard this from me, and I won't corroborate anything you say about the matter."

"Understood. But why should I give you her

address?"

"Because I need to replace her bike, and I need to apologise. Please Eve, I want to make this right with her. If you won't give me her address, at least give me her phone number and then she can make her own decision whether she sees me or not."

"You hurt her again and you'll discover just what a makeup artist does when seeking revenge, big Hollywood star or not. And Tom, you had better make it right with her, I've just taken her back on my team and I want her to do your makeup on Ironclaw."

I fist bumped the air. I had no intention of hurting Jane. Although the thought of Eve taking revenge made me grimace as I thought back to a rumour, I once heard about how a minor actor had indecently proposed to a member of Eve's staff and disappeared for a month. It was said she had painted a cock on his face, and it had taken that long to get it off.

"It was an accident, Eve. I never meant to knock her off her bike. We are friends."

"Friends? Have you even spoken to her in the last six months?" she asked.

"I never knew she was leaving. I never had a contact for her. I don't even know her last name." Of course, I didn't add, I never knew her first name either.

"It's Bennett, Tom and alright, I'll give you her number but then it's up to her whether she speaks to you or not."

CHAPTER 16

BETH

When I returned home later that night, the only thing I wanted to do was immerse myself in a nice, soothing bath. But when I opened the door. Hunter was standing with his back to me, stark bollock naked, a man kneeling at his feet, one hand on his arse.

"For fuck's sake, Hunter, couldn't you have taken this into the bedroom?" I exclaimed, throwing my handbag on the sofa.

He didn't even flinch, just craned his head around and frowned. "Is everything alright, Beth? It's not like you to swear."

He didn't even comment on what I was wearing. I raised my hands, gestured to his nakedness, and shrugged my shoulders. Look on the bright side Beth, I reminded myself; Hunter's rear view was pretty impressive, and few girls were lucky enough to see it.

"Oh, it's not what it looks like. It's art," he said. I raised an eyebrow; I didn't think Hunter was gullible. "Alfonso is doing a cast of my jewels. It's for the club. Kind of homage to our manliness. Come have a look poppet, then I can give you a hug. You look like you could do with one."

My hands dropped. What the heck, I thought, studying his tight buns. I shuffled over to the pair, and Hunter wrapped an arm around my shoulders.

"Shit day, honey?" he asked.

I nodded and then shook my head, wrapping my arm around his waist. I hung on as though I was a child and he, my giant teddy bear.

"What do you think?" Hunter asked, gesturing to his groin where Alfonso daubed on a thick white paste. There was something sensual about watching him work.

As my gaze trailed down to his foam-covered banana split, my eyes widened. I knew Hunter was an impressive physical specimen, but Holy Moly.

"That's you at ease, soldier?" I asked.

Hunter smirked. "Ah ha."

"And everyone's comfortable being on display when they're compared to that?" I asked.

"Oh, it will be anonymous. But I'm not the largest," he said.

My hand slid subconsciously down to his bum and massaged it. "You're not? Then who is?"

"Lola."

"Lola, you're kidding me?"

"I kid you not. And Beth, stop massaging my behind. You're going to see this sergeant stand to attention if you carry on."

"Oh, I'm sorry, Hunter, I don't know what came over

me?" I flushed as red as a smacked behind.

"It's okay. I have that effect on people. Although, to be fair, women rarely have that effect on me." He glanced down at his cock. I tried not to follow his gaze down to his salute, but Mont Blanc was too much of a draw. "Has anyone told you that you have a wonderful touch? You really need to put those hands to good use and get a boyfriend, sugar."

My eyes misted, and I swallowed down a sobbing choke.

"Hey, what's this all about?"

"I saw Tom today. He knocked me off my bike, I mean yours, outside the studio and then hugged me and called me a bitch. It was hideously embarrassing. I can't talk about it now; I need a bath."

"Okay cherub, go have a bath and we'll talk later. Love you."

In fact, we didn't speak of it until the next morning. I hadn't even made it as far as the bathroom. When my legs wobbled, my heart dipped, and a tsunami of emotion ploughed through me like a breaker smashing through arctic ice. Hunter woke me in the morning bearing a cup of tea and his version of a heartbreak breakfast. Strawberries, chocolate hobnobs, yoghurt and a flaming Sambuca on the side. I grinned up at him and patted the bed.

"Fuck, you look awful. What did he knock you off your bike with, a sledgehammer? No wait, looking like that, it must have been Thor's hammer?"

"It was his Range Rover's door." I took a biscuit and

nibbled it experimentally. "I don't want to look in the mirror. Am I really hideous?"

"No more than usual, hun. You just look as if you've been cage fighting with Anderson 'The Spider' Silva."

"Who?" I asked.

Hunter rolled his eyes. "Oh, for goodness' sake, don't you know anything? Anderson "The Spider" Silva is the greatest MMA of all time." He looked at me like my junior teacher had, when he asked me when lunch was, and I replied, 'when the bell rings'. He continued, "Brazilian born Silva holds the title for the longest title reign in history! He's an expert in boxing, judo, Jujitsu, Taekwondo and Capoeira.

"Why do they call him 'The Spider'?" I asked.

"I don't bloody know."

I gave him a nudge. "But you do, don't you?"

"Of course I do, but I never came here to talk about mixed martial arts. I came to get the gossip about what went down yesterday with the gorgeous Tom Austin aka Edward Rochester."

"I've already told you. I went down like a sack of potatoes at his feet." I narrowed my eyes. "How do you know I refer to him as Mr Rochester?"

"You talk in your sleep."

I nodded, then did a double take. We had separate rooms.

"Don't digress. What happened?" he said, waving his hands about.

"I was cycling to my meeting with Eve and his door opened. I swerved and crashed into the pavement. Tom dragged me to my feet, apologising profusely, we went to pick my bike up, we banged heads, I blew off, he hugged me and then he called me a bitch... and walked off." My lip trembled.

You can take a breath, Jane. "Wait, did you say you farted?"

My face heated until I was sure my hair would catch fire. "Yes, I was nervous!"

He chuckled.

"I don't think he heard or smelt it. I did a check. It was barely noticeable." My forehead crinkled as I replayed our conversation back in my head.

Hunter roared with laughter. "I bet he did."

"Okay, he did." I admitted. "He told me I blew a hole in my leggings." I dropped my head, grabbed the Sambuca and downed it in one; it was a Saturday, after all.

"That's a good thing. He made light of it, to show you he didn't care."

"Then, if you're right, why did he walk off and call me a bitch?"

Hunter frowned. "That is puzzling. Go have a bath and I'll have a think about it."

***

When I got out of the bath, Susie and Hunter were standing in the kitchen drinking Sambuca. Silence fell as

I walked in.

"What?" I asked. Contrary to what you might have thought, Sambuca was not our usual Saturday morning beverage - tea was.

Susie looked at Hunter. "You show her. She's used to receiving bad news from you."

"Don't throw me under the bus, just because I'm a straight talker! I might have picked up her phone and berated her boyfriend, wrongly it appears, so you should show her." Hunter pushed a newspaper into Susie's chest, who fumbled with it like it was a hot potato.

"Hang on guys, what on earth is going on?" I asked.

Susie grimaced. "The good news is you're in the papers, and a beloved Disney character."

Hunter tutted and rolled his eyes.

"I'm breaking it to her gently." She snapped.

"You're drawing it out. Be kind, pull the tooth in one sharp motion!"

"I can't. It will break her."

I looked wide eyed, from one to the other.

Hunter snatched up the paper and held it out so I could see the headline. "Beauty Slays the Beast!"

It took a moment for the article to sink in. Not that it was difficult to figure out which one was which.

Hunter held out his finger. "I just had a lightbulb moment!"

I stood numb, my heart thundering against my ribs. Tom looked so heroic, and I looked – like I imagined I would - hideous.

"What's your lightbulb moment, Hunter? I think Beth needs to hear it now. It had better be good news," Susie said.

I didn't even ask why everyone was talking as though I wasn't in the room. It seemed normal that they should. I could barely tell if I was standing before them – it was as if I was in a parallel universe, and I stood before them as a fuzzy hologram.

"Beth, he never called you a bitch. Don't you see? He saw who took the picture, and it was them he was speaking to."

"Oh, that will make her feel much better, Hunter. Being branded the beast in a national newspaper in front of the guy she has a massive crush on is the boost to her self-confidence she needs."

"It does actually," I said. My mind clicked back into action. "Hunter, you said you berated my boyfriend this morning. How could you have done that when I haven't got one?"

Hunter and Susie exchanged looks until she nodded. "Tom rang your mobile this morning to see how you were. I rejected the call, and then he rang again. I told him an actual friend would have replied to the butchered bunnies. He said he didn't know what I was talking about. So, I hung up, and then Karen rang. She'd seen the news online." He exhaled. "She said she never gave Tom the letter. That it was all a mix up and that she was sorry, and she'd tell you what happened when she returned to England next month."

"And Tom?"

"He rang again, but the paper had just arrived."

I held my breath.

"He's going to come over in an hour. He wanted to come straight away, but I told him no. We needed time to break the news to you gently."

Susie snorted, and I laughed.

***

The next hour was an hour of paradoxes, made up of portions of time that travelled as if composed of segments, where a few minutes appeared to pass at the wrong speed, like a 78-record playing at 33 rpm, So, it... went... very... slowly, and then quite the reverse.

Looking at the newspaper headline drew me in until I resembled a gnat encased in amber. Fascinated by the catastrophe before me, I stared at the image of my face as though by staring at it, I could cast a magic spell until I, the beautiful princess, lay at the handsome princes' feet. Alas, no amount of gazing made the slightest bit of difference. There was no spell to be made or broken that would change this beast into anything other than what it was.

After staring at my slumped form, for what was perhaps minutes but felt like hours, my vision moved onto Tom's and the opposite happened. But then, the man looked nothing other than what he was in photographs – too hot.

"Beth, snap out of it! Get yourself into that bathroom and put on your face, for heaven's sake. He'll be here any minute!" Hunter said.

I scrabbled to my feet and made my way into the bathroom. Whacked on some deodorant and raked a brush through my hair. Halfway through brushing my teeth, I glanced in the mirror and paused. What the hell was I doing? The Beast only got her beauty in fairy tales or works of fiction, like when Jane got her Mr Rochester – admittedly, not until he was hideously scarred, and his mansion burnt to the ground. And for a second, I pictured Tom tragically maimed in a car accident, his career in tatters, the bevy of beauties that once hung on his arm a distant dream and me, his consolation, his booby prize, the one he'd settled for because he had become a beast too. But then, who but a psychopath would want that to happen to the man of their dreams? Yes, alright, I pictured it briefly. Everyone had a right to the occasional warped fantasy, but I really didn't want that to happen just so I stood a chance with him. Did I? No, I'm kidding. No one wanted to see a Greek tragedy here!

Friends. That was as much as I could hope for and if I was lucky, one day my heart wouldn't flutter when someone mentioned his name. I would be overjoyed to be the respectable maiden aunt to his beautiful children, and his wife would confide in me that it drove her mad when he left the toilet seat up or his dirty pants for the cleaner to put in the laundry basket.

I dressed in jeans and a t-shirt that read "Free for fifty quid", an odd choice perhaps, but I liked the irony. Hunter barged into my room, flapping his hands about as if he was squatting flies.

"He'll be here any minute! Get a move on! Beth, why haven't you done your face?"

"You've heard the saying, you can't polish a turd, haven't you?" I asked.

"Beth, you don't give yourself enough credit. He already likes you."

"He likes me, yes, but that was before he knew what I looked like, and what do you think I'm taking credit for, that I'm the Beast of Bermondsey, not Bodmin? Neither makes me beautiful."

Hunter pursed his lips. "Put some mascara on and a bit of lip balm, or I'll tell him you're my girlfriend and to take a hike! Hell, I might do it anyway. It won't hurt at all to see one hot guy after your arse. It can only encourage him — bees to honey and all that."

"Hunter, no! Please don't do that," I said, putting my hands together.

"Why not? You want this guy, don't you?"

"He'll never believe you're going out with me anymore than he'd care who I go out with."

Hunter shuffled along beside me on my dressing table stool and took up my mascara. Taking hold of my chin, he guided the mascara wand across my lashes and said, "Look, hun, looks aren't everything." He pressed his finger to my lips. "Really, they aren't. He obviously already likes you enough to be checking whether you're alright. And you ain't that ugly! To tell you the truth, hun, if I wasn't gay, I'd shag you. Especially after that bum massage the other day." He smirked. "You're not up for a threesome, are you?"

"Hunter!"

"I'm joking!" he said. "But if you ever change your mind." He winked. "Seriously, the guy is probably sick to the teeth with all these beautiful high maintenance chicks he has little in common with. Can you imagine always fighting someone for room in front of the mirror? Don't get me wrong, you have to find someone attractive, but attraction isn't all about perfection, it's about friendship, trust and fun as well."

I wrapped my arms around Hunter and gazed up into his handsome face. "No, I can't imagine what it would be like vying for the mirror."

"No, you wouldn't, would you? You're the only makeup artist I know who rarely looks in a mirror at herself."

"I'm proud of you Hunter, who knew you had a wise head on that ridiculously sculpted frame." I reached up and kissed his chin just as Susie opened my bedroom door. In the background, Tom stood, holding the handlebars of a shiny new bike. My heart gave a leap, and I squeezed my arms tighter around Hunter and stared.

CHAPTER 17

TOM

It took me an age in the cycle shop to choose a bike for Jane. I tried to recall what the one she was riding had looked like, but only came up with a blank. Jane's face jumped into my mind. It was the first time I'd seen her stripped down to her chassis, and the first thing I'd noticed was her ankles. Jane had ankles a finely crafted Chippendale would be proud of, and the rest of her legs, in fact, her entire figure, had enough womanly curves to make me take a second look. She hadn't a model's figure with legs up to her armpits, but whoa, Jane had been hiding assets behind those baggy bright garments she usually wore and for a while I forgot where I was and what I was supposed to do. And then my gaze alighted on her face, and I smiled. It suited her perfectly, chestnut hair, warm amber eyes, a pale skin, rosy cheeks. Jane may not have been a great beauty, but she was like finding a cool spring on a hot summer's day or picking a fruit, small and like all the other apples on the tree but sweet and juicy, which overflowing into your mouth. And after only one bite, you had to eat the entire thing.

Eventually I got out my phone and scrolled to the newspaper article to see if I could figure out the crumpled mess on the pavement, but it only made me grind my teeth and frightened the sales assistant into giving me a wide berth. As I walked up and down the rows of bicycles, I settled on a silver racer style town bike with a basket on the front, a tiny rose emblem on the cross bars caught my eye and it was enough to remind me of Jane's quirkiness to want to buy it for her. I made sure it had lights and a bell before I left the shop and put it in the back of my Range Rover.

A guy called Hunter answered the phone when I'd rung and quickly made it clear he thought I wasn't worth Jane's time. I hoped this was because he was a good friend or her brother, or at least acting in a brotherly fashion. But what if he was the guy Karen had told me about, the one who was having fun in her bedroom?

Approaching a junction, I clunked my gearbox into second gear and called an old fella using a crossing like a snail on sand a few choice words. Before I caught myself scowling in the mirror and tried to relax my shoulders.

Jane never had a boyfriend, or so she told me six months ago, I reminded myself. Why would she have one now? Why wouldn't she? Jane was a hidden gem, my subconscious told me. And hidden gems were made to be uncovered just as sure as treasure buried on a desert island under a big, black bugger of a cross was. You ass!

So, I stood at her door and waited while a woman, who wasn't Jane, opened it and ushered me in. There was barely room for both the bike and me. I wondered where she had kept her old one as there didn't appear to be anywhere to put it. Susie, the woman who opened the door, gave me a breezy smile and walked over to a pink door, adorned with a winking eye shaded in multi-coloured eyeshadow. It was extraordinary; Jane had to have been the one responsible for the makeup, it screamed "Plain Jane did this".

When Susie flung Jane's door wide open, I suddenly had the sensation I was falling through a stage trap door, plummeting into a deep hole of darkness where the bottom was nowhere in sight. I gripped onto the handlebars tighter and widened my stance.

The guy Jane was kissing looked over her head and smirked. He hadn't moved his hands from around her waist, but I swear he wrote a one up on you, buddy sign in the air above her head.

Jane turned and stared at me. I think she even pulled the guy in tighter to her embrace. I frowned as something contracted in my chest. The bike clattered to the floor; in the constricted space, the pedal whacked my ankle, and I hopped, reached down, and hugged it. Jane's eyebrows rose as I lost my balance and disappeared behind their sofa with an enormous thud, a cloud of sparkly dust and a barrage of "Fuck!", "Bugger it!", "Blasted buggering fuck!".

Her roommate gasped and peeked around the sofa. I glared at her as she stepped back. Jane and the guy peered over the back of the sofa, her mouth open in a wide O. The guy chuckled.

"Looks like he's fallen for you!" he said.

My eyes snapped from Jane's to his, my mouth a tight white line. I guessed the guy was Hunter, a stupid name. The jerk was incredibly handsome, grinning as if he was a fox in a chicken coop and I was a hen. Wait, that's a crazy analogy. Whatever the case, I was outside the coop, hanging onto the wire, wanting in, to raid it and claim the dowdy, but desirable hen, and all-round good egg.

"Are you okay?" Jane asked.

"Is he your boyfriend?" I replied.

Jane looked over at Hunter, then back at me. "We're friends."

"Good friends," Hunter said, his head nodding, with an upturned lip curling the corner of his mouth.

I scowled and rose to my feet, hobbling as I tried to put weight on the injured ankle.

"I brought you a new bike," I said.

Jane glanced down at the silver ladies' bike with the small rose on it and grinned. "Thank you, Tom, that was very kind of you, but it didn't belong to me. I borrowed it from a male friend of mine. Do you think you could swap it for a men's?"

"You have another male friend?" I could have punched myself. Why did I say that?

"Yes, quite a few, Mr Rochester."

I frowned. "Are you making fun of me, Jane?"

She smiled softly. "A little. Let's take a look at that ankle, shall we?"

I glared and let her guide me around to the sofa. "Sit," Jane said.

Then she looked at her friends and, thanks to some kind of silent communication, Hunter said, "Come on Susie, let's go for a coffee at the corner shop." Susie stood and stared, her mouth ajar. "Sues, this way." He guided her by the arm to the door. She followed him meekly as a lamb.

"You don't have to leave, you know?" Jane said.

Hunter stood the bike up and propped it against the wall. "I know, but you two need some space. We won't be long. Text me if you need us." Hunter looked over at me. "I'll give you the benefit of the doubt this time, but if you hurt my girl, Hollywood star or not, I'll make your ex-girlfriend look like Shirley Temple."

I nodded and watched the door close. Jane came over with some ice wrapped in a tea cloth and sat beside me and rolled up my trouser leg. I couldn't drag my gaze from her face after so long of not knowing what she looked like. I wanted to drink in every feature as though I was sitting in front of a canvas, unremarkable, but held transfixed, until every other painting in the gallery disappeared.

As she put ice on my bruised shin, I grimaced.

"Sorry, it will help take the swelling down," she said, smiling with a faint tint of rose to her cheeks. Just above her eyebrow was a vivid purple bruise. I brushed a finger around it, pushing her fringe back.

"Are you well, Jane?"

"Yes sir, only achy and bruised, but fine," she said, her gaze meeting mine.

"What about the headline?"

She gave a small shrug. "Was it Alisha?"

"Yes." I shuffled in my seat until we were eye to eye. "It's all rubbish, you know that, don't you?"

I watched her eyelashes flutter and a sheen coat her eyes. She smiled.

"You are not a beast, Jane. It's nonsense. Just a vicious ex of mine who wants to hurt those around me."

Jane nodded. "Bullies pick on easy targets don't they? She hasn't picked on any other acquaintance of yours. I know because I've followed you in the papers." Her head dropped; her concentration focused on my ankle. "I wanted to know how the man I considered a friend was doing. Whether he was well and why he never…"

"Said goodbye or answered your letter?" I finished for her.

"I don't know why you ever would?" she said as a smile played around her lips.

"I'm sorry, but I never got the letter, and I thought about contacting you. I wanted to, but then-"

"Why would you?" She interrupted me. "I'm nothing to you, nor would I expect to be. Our lives are totally different."

"No, that isn't true. I wanted to stay friends, but I only knew you as Jane and when I asked Karen, she told me a friend would already have your number."

A silence fell and then she reached a hand towards me, and my pulse throbbed.

"Alright then, give me your phone."

I fumbled in my pocket. Finding it, I brought it out and watched as she tapped in her number.

"Now you've got it. No more excuses Rochester, for not keeping in touch."

I grinned. "Great. I'll text you and then you'll have my number. Do you ride?"

"Rather an impertinent question!" she said.

I flushed. "I meant horse riding. Would you like to go horse riding with me?"

She narrowed her eyes. "Did you hit your head when you fell?"

I was beginning to wonder the same thing. "No, I don't think so? I just enjoyed it and wondered if you did too? If not, I could teach you or we could do something else?"

"Okay?"

"I miss the countryside, the freedom, the lack of press. It will give us a chance to talk without interruption."

Jane's face screwed up in thought as she absentmindedly stroked my leg. I groaned. Her gaze flitted to my face, and I grinned.

"You still haven't lost your touch. If it works on horses, you could become the next horse whisperer."

She snorted, her face pink as a salmon sky, and we both laughed.

"I've missed you." I confessed, dropping my gaze. "Well, I think I had better be going," I said, getting up.

She rose and bit her lip, then reached a hand up to stroke my jaw. I leaned down to her and brushed my lips over hers. A jolt of electricity flowed between us, and I took a step back. Why did I kiss Jane? It was only a peck between friends; I reminded myself, running my tongue over where her lips had touched mine. Blast! Horse whisperer my foot! I was the one wearing a bridle, and I couldn't wait until she put on a saddle and took me for a ride.

I limped to the door and opened it. Jane took the handlebars and wheeled the bike to the car, watching me as I lifted it in.

"What type of bike did your friend have?" I asked, eager for the moment to last.

"I'm not sure. Can I text you when I find out what it was? I haven't ridden for years." Her face coloured, and I wondered what that meant.

"So, you're up for a ride in the country at the weekend, say, Saturday at ten sharp?"

"I haven't any riding boots or a hat or anything," Jane said.

"It's okay, my friend can lend you some. Text me what size feet you have, and I'll sort it."

"Alright, it's a date." She waved her hands about. "I didn't mean a date, date. You know what I meant."

"Yes, yes, of course." I turned my back and pulled a face. Why couldn't I have just said it was a date? I was behaving like a teenager, not a Hollywood heartthrob, who'd dated loads of beautiful women without them even raising my heart rate and now it was hammering away as if someone was banging a big bass drum.

CHAPTER 18

BETH

I sat on the sofa and listened as Susie and Hunter scrabbled at the front door. They were giggling so hard; they couldn't find the keyhole. As soon as they were inside, they fell silent as they came to sit beside me.

"Is he here?" Susie whispered.

I raised an eyebrow. "Where do you think he might be?" I asked, looking around the open plan, kitchen, lounge diner.

"In the bathroom?" Susie replied.

I looked over to it and said, "The door's open, Sues?"

"In your bedroom tied to your headboard?" Hunter smirked and winked at Susie.

I rolled my eyes. In my wildest dreams, I thought. "Sorry to disappoint, but no."

"Oh, so he's left already? You never gave him anything?"

Hunter tittered as I threw him a dirty look. He put his hands in the air and cried, "What? I didn't say anything?"

"It's what you implied. He only popped around to drop off the bike."

"We know he said that but… Let's face it, a man as famous as him could have sent a minion to do that. So, what else did he say?" Susie asked as she leaned forward in her seat.

"He asked me to go riding with him on Saturday."

"That's all very formal. I've never made a date for a shag like that in my life! It must be the posh boy in him," Hunter said.

"Oh please! You can't help lowering the tone, can you, Hunter? It's not that type of riding, it's horse riding."

"You know how to ride a horse?" Susie asked.

Distracted by Hunter's quip, I only shrugged, trying not to think how sore my legs were going to be after Saturday.

"Oh, horse riding is a euphemism for a roll in the hay now, is it?"

"Hunter, when are you going to get it? We are just friends. Nothing else. It's never going to happen, not in a million trillion years. It would be like an Arab stallion with Thelwell's pony."

"What's Thelwell's pony?" Susie asked.

"It's a cartoon Shetland pony," Hunter and I replied at the same time.

Susie and I looked at him and raised our eyebrows. What did he know about horses?

"What? You don't think I'm restricted to one type of

stallion," he said with a wink.

I put my hand up. "Too much information Hunter, I don't want to know about your beastly pursuits. I mean yuck, just ew, stop right there!" I mimicked, throwing up as Susie chuckled.

"No, no, not that kind of riding. I meant horse riding! I used to go horse riding." He insisted. "I'm not that much of a pervert!"

"That's not what I heard," Susie teased. We exchanged looks and fell about laughing.

Hunter shook his head. "Absolutely not!"

"Of course, that's what you meant!" I said. "But with your track record, we'd believe you were capable of anything." I snorted, tears of laughter rolling down my face.

Hunter poked me in the ribs and cuffed an arm around Susie's neck. "Right, you two are going to get it!"

"Both of us at the same time? You're more talented than we thought!" I tickled his stomach, and while he was wriggling like a worm. Susie took advantage and wrestled him to the floor.

"Get his wrists!" She cried, straddling him while tickling him at the same time.

"No, no! Stop! Stop, you're going to pay for this!" Hunter squirmed and bucked under Susie's ample behind and was powerless to do anything but laugh and thrash. "Help! Help! Anyone help, they're killing me!" He shrieked.

"Gag him! He'll have the neighbours beating down

the door at any minute! You big Jess, Hunter, crying over two girls whipping your ass!"

"Oh, promises, promises!" Hunter threw out between crying and laughing as I whipped off a sock and shoved it into his mouth. Hunter's face went bright red, and Susie and I braced ourselves. This was the bit where he had enough of playing the victim and went all Hulk on us. He tightened his muscles, spat the sock out of his mouth and roared, "I have the power!"

Okay, that was He-man, but the Hulk was pretty nonverbal, so compromises had to be made. He heaved Susie up into the air as though she were riding a bucking bronco and tensed his fists, releasing his hands. In one move he had Susie flat on her back with her legs waving in the air as though she was an upturned beetle and had me braced between his thighs, my hair splayed out around me like a snow angel. He then tickled us both with his fingers, mouth, and hair until tears streaked down our faces and we hiccupped breathlessly with laughter. We were probably getting too old for this kind of horseplay, but none of us was complaining. Oh, we begged for him to stop, but it was cry wolf, and when Susie squealed, she was going to pee herself he let her have a toilet break but tackled her when she got back and threw her onto our sofa, while I jumped onto his back. Both us girls complained the sofa was brand new and needed to be shown some respect, but in reply, all Hunter did was roar, "Respect, you wenches, show me some respect and I won't have to reprimand you!"

We dived back into the fray as though we were WWE tag team wrestlers.

Ten minutes later, we were breathless, sweaty, and

sporting a few bruises and had decided it was time for a nice cup of tea and a cherry Bakewell.

"That was so much fun," Hunter declared, rubbing his hip. "No revealing outfits for me Saturday night at the club, though, or one of the punters will ring Child Line."

Susie and I burst into laughter; Hunter was such an idiot and, of course, we weren't even as remotely as childish.

"You really are a fool. How many hours a day do you have to practise?" Susie asked.

"Ha ha. I take the art of playing the clown extremely serious, and you girls need a bit of excitement in your lives. Just think what it would be like without me as your flat mate and best friend?"

"Boring, and dull as dishwater darling," I said.

"Exactly! So, what are you going to wear Saturday while 'horse riding' Beth?" Hunter asked.

"Jeans and a t-shirt, and I'll probably take a jacket. Why?"

Hunter choked on his cake. "You have to ask? What if he suggests lunch on the way home and lunch leads to other things?" He waggled his eyebrows up and down. Susie snorted as I gave her a reproving stare.

"We are only friends!" I huffed. "Alright, I'd like more, but I'm the beast of Bermondsey. Can you really see that working out?"

Susie, bless her, shook her head, no. She knew what it was like to be the fat kid in school. There was no way she'd give me false hope. Hunter glared at her and nodded his head.

"I know about these things!" he declared. "He might have spent all his life chasing the pedigree, but he's got the scent of a mongrel and his senses are in a whirl. Pretty soon, he'll stop chasing his tail and chase yours instead."

"Hunter, what did you have to call Beth a mongrel for? So, is that how you see us as mongrels and you're a poncey pedigree?" she said, fisting her hand tightly.

"Tom and I aren't just pedigrees, we're Crufts's best of breed prize winners, and I'm going to say it again like I've said it before, it's not all about looks, it's about, trust, companionship, fun, compatibility and plain old chemistry! Perfection is highly overrated and almost always an illusion."

I looked at his expression and frowned. This was a side to him I rarely saw. Then it occurred to me that Hunter might also be interested in someone that wasn't his normal kind of beau.

"Have you got your eye on a Plain Jane as well?" I asked, taking hold of his hand.

"No, there's nothing plain about Liam, and I suspect Tom would say the same thing about you, Beth."

"Liam? Who's Liam?" I asked.

Susie sat forward in her seat and leaned her elbows on the table. "Do tell, Hunter. Come on, who's this mysterious Liam?"

"What, you haven't heard of him before either, Susie?" I asked.

Hunter rolled his eyes. "You're like vultures picking

at a carcass."

"Oh, this is going to be good. You're serious about this guy, aren't you? What is he like? Is he an underwear model or a professional sportsman, all rippling muscles and designer stubble?" Susie asked.

"No, he is not!"

"Okay, Hunter, so what is he like?" I asked, patting his hand.

"Liam is incredible, intelligent, strong, kind, sexy, thoughtful, domineering and not mine."

Susie's mouth dropped open. She took one look at me and pulled a face, mouthing, 'What does he mean? Not mine?'

I gave Hunter's hand a squeeze and asked, "So, he's not gay, then?"

This was the only explanation I could come up with for Hunter's lack of success with Liam. He always got his man. I knew everyone had a type they went for, but experience had shown us he was everyone's type. Including a few 'straight' married men's, black, oriental and those visiting from another universe.

Hunter was a chameleon; he could do the rough biker look, the smooth, sophisticated, well-manicured model look, the happy hippie, free love, and everything in between. Hunter loved to be loved, and I know what you're thinking. Had the real Hunter got lost in all these transformations? Out in public, yes, but at home he was just Hunter and as gorgeous as himself as any other clone.

Hunter shook his head. "It's not that."

"What do you mean by that?" Susie asked.

I glanced between the pair of them, my face screwed up in thought.

"Why has he turned you down, Hunter?" I asked.

"He hasn't. At least that's what he said the other day. He said he'll ask me when he wants to and in his own time, that whiney little boys like me don't get to pull the shots."

Susie swallowed. "Oh, are you sure you want to date this guy?"

"God, yes! I don't want to just date him. He's everything to me. The whole shebang, the one and only."

"Hunter?" I asked, gripping his hand tightly as he gazed into my eyes. "How do you know that if you've never dated?"

"Because we're friends and we've been friends for the last five years. He knows everything about me, and I know him, and we go together perfectly, like an egg yolk and the white that surrounds it."

"The albumen?" I replied vaguely, wondering which was which. I guessed Liam was the yolk? "How come we don't know him?"

"You do. Only you know him as Lola."

"The dwarf with the big schlong?" Susie gasped.

Hunter pursed his lips. "He's a person foremost, Susan."

"Sorry, but he is a dwarf. I'm only speaking the truth, and you told me he was endowed like a horse. Isn't that how you put it?"

His frown deepened. "And if someone described you as the fat bird who eats too many cakes, that would be alright, would it? That would sum up all that you are and everything people see when they first meet you!"

I grabbed Susie's hand as her lip trembled. It wasn't like him to be cruel, and although I could see his point, I knew this would be like an arrow to her chest.

"Hunter, you know Susie has wrestled with her weight since she was a child," I said.

"Yes, I do Beth, and I also know that she's fat because of bad eating habits taught by her parents, but it's not something she can't change. She has a choice whether she's fat or not. Unlike Liam, who was born that way and has to live with the stigma and taunts all his life and can't do a damn thing about it!"

Susie gripped my hand tight, and I closed my eyes, ready for the barrage of insults to start.

"It's alright for you looking like a Greek god, Hunter. You don't know what it's like to be anything other than perfect! And how could you say that about choice, when you know how many diets I've been on, trying to shed the pounds over the years?"

"You could actually follow the diet, Susie, if you really wanted to lose the pounds, instead of reading about what you should do and carrying on as normal. Beth and I know you've read more slimming books than you've had cooked dinners, and let's face it, you've had more than your fair share of those."

"At least I'm honest about myself, unlike you, who

changes yourself at a drop of a hat because you're so desperate for love. But it's not working is it, because you're still alone! You're a fake Hunter Brando. So fake. I bet that isn't even your real name! And now, not only are you a fraud, you're scraping the bottom of the barrel and prepared to go out with an ugly midget! I may be fat, but at least I have a boyfriend who loves me for myself and not some trumped up reason!"

"Sues!" I gasped, dropping hold of her hand. I stepped closer to Hunter – Susie was about to go nuclear and what resulted wouldn't be pretty.

"What? Oh, I know how pally pally you've got with him and now he's filling your head with hopeless dreams of you and Tom Austin together! As if. It's never gonna happen in this century, Beth. Listen to a proper friend who will tell you the truth and not fill your head with stupid fantasies; Tom Austin will never be your boyfriend! As for you, Hunter, I'm not surprised your poisoned dwarf won't go out with you. You don't even know who you are!" She took a breath as every muscle in my body tightened. "Well, I do, you primped up prima donna, who's no better than that pathetic plastic doll that twists round and round on her pedestal performing for an audience that doesn't care and forgets she even exists the second they drop the lid on that cheap, tacky box she lives in! Hunter Brando, you're nothing! You're less than nothing! You're as substantial as a cloud, paper thin, and meaningless. As insignificant as a maggot on roadkill. As worthy as the dirt on my shoe! The dregs from a soil pipe, the spittle from a toothless drunkard's cracked lip, the sperm that missed the egg!"

Hunter recoiled as Susie turned around and headed

for the door, closing it gently like a whisper of breath after a hurricane. It was her trademark. When Susie blew, everyone ducked for cover. It was rare and lethal, like a laser burning through paper.

Hunter stood, a hand to his chest, tears in his eyes. His face crumpled as my heart dipped.

"I'm sure she never meant everything she said. You know how she gets when you stroke her temper, but she doesn't mean it, I'm sure." I laid a hand on his arm.

He barked, a peculiar sound I couldn't determine just what it was. Something between a sob, a hiccup, and a laugh. "Hunter?" I asked, rubbing his arm briskly.

"Fuck me! That girl really doesn't like being called fat, does she?" He bent over and belly laughed at his feet. "The sperm that missed the egg! I never realised Sues was so talented with words!"

"You don't mind that she called Liam ugly or you a fake?"

"No, because he's not, although calling me fake stung a bit, it's true though, and they say the truth hurts. Well, it does, like a knife to the gut, but hey, live by the sword, die by the sword! And I did call her fat, so touché, a blade for a blade." He straightened, wiping tears of laughter from his face.

We sat at the table, and Hunter took his phone out. He held up the screen and showed me a picture of a very handsome man.

"Who's that?" I asked, squinting at the image. There was something familiar about him, but I couldn't figure out what.

"That's Liam," Hunter said, kissing the screen.

"Liam? The same Liam who works at the Trap door and goes under the drag name of Lola?"

"Yep, he makes an ugly drag queen, doesn't he? His face is too strong, too masculine, just like Tom's, too male to pass as a decent female."

I nodded, dumbfounded, unable to take my eyes off the screen.

"You could say I'm the Plain Jane in this situation, Beth, and it's worse than that because I'm also an insignificant fake, no better than a maggot on roadkill." Hunter grinned.

"So, why are you smiling?"

"Because Susie doesn't know shit! You and I sister are going to get our man." He winked.

"Apparently not in this century. If she's right, I could be the oldest woman in history if your prediction is true."

"There's a bright side to every cloud, Beth. Although I don't believe you'll have to wait that long. Trust me; shitty-coloured, maggot shaped, ethereal clouds, know about these things."

CHAPTER 19

TOM

I got in my car and drove away from Jane's, and as soon as I was around the corner, I floored the accelerator and whooped. Jane and I were going riding – horse riding, I reminded myself. What other riding would I be interested in with Jane, anyway? I mean, we were just friends; I didn't like her that way. Then I thought of her smile and the way her eyes twinkled when she teased me, and the way her hands skittered over my skin as goosebumps raised in anticipation of her touch and my body primed as though it was a torpedo, in its chamber ready to launch. Well, I couldn't deny it any longer – my attraction was as vivid and alive as flames dancing in a fire. If I was honest, I was fanning them more than I'd fanned any before in my life.

It then struck me that Jane hadn't seemed overly keen, Hunter could still be her boyfriend, and I didn't know her real name apart from Bennet, but I couldn't call her that! I braked hard. Someone behind me screeched to a stop and leaned on their horn. The bike clattered into the seats and came to rest at a jaunty angle. I had the good sense to place a cap on my head and dip my head as the driver behind me swerved around my car and gave me the bird out of his open window. With any luck, he wouldn't have recognised me.

"Stupid bloody posh twat!" they shouted from the window.

I growled and gripped the steering wheel tight. Sometimes fame was a bind. It steadied your normal reactions, made you think before you gestured back or told someone to get lost. At least, someone with my reputation did. Okay, Johnny Depp or Oliver Reed got away with it most of the time, but then, allegedly, the demon drink was to blame. That was one reason I rarely drank. I couldn't afford to lose control and the other was this former fat boy liked to eat and I couldn't afford to eat and drink and remain a Hollywood hunk. And I'd been a fat boy long enough to know that I wasn't in a tearing hurry to regain the title.

Of course, Jane wasn't fat, unlike her chubby flat mate, but she was… unremarkably remarkable. I reached a hand up to my head. Had I hit it when the bike attacked me?

By the time I walked into my apartment, my phone pinged. I glanced down and grinned. The message was from Jane, and it said, *"Dear Mr Rochester, I fear my friend is taking liberties. They claim the bike you trashed was a S-WORKS Turbo something. I'll send you the link. Feel free to tell them to run with their leg up. Jane."*

Buoyed by her rapid response, I tapped out a reply without following the link. *"No problem. I'll order it after I've walked Drago. PS. He missed you, too. R"*

"A fool and their money," she replied.

I grabbed Drago's lead off the side and whistle for

him to come. He bounded up to me, waggling his tail, and grabbed the lead, while I tapped on the link and gasped. "Fuck! Eleven grand!" I looked at Drago as he dropped the lead he was holding in his mouth and turned his head to one side. "I laughed. This friend of hers saw me coming! I thought I was being generous when I bought her one for four hundred!"

I grabbed my phone and typed in. *"Eleven grand!"* Big eyed emoji.

The phone beeped. *"You never followed the link, did you? They're not that good a friend of mine. Tell them to get stuffed! The greedy pig is barely one payslip away from living in a cardboard box. There's no way they could afford a bike like that!"*

"They're a good enough friend for you to know their financial position?"

"Yes, well, they don't need you to provide them with a lottery win. I can tell you now, they'll sell it, buy a cheap one and waste the rest on designer frocks and Dolly Parton-style wigs. Keep your hands in your pocket, Mr Rochester, they're safest there."

"What type of friend buys designer frocks and big wigs?"

"My flatmate, Hunter, he's a drag queen."

I thought about the handsome guy with the designer eyebrows Jane had her hands on and her lips when I walked in with the bike and grinned.

"And Hunter's…?" Would it be rude of me to ask if he was gay? It would be my luck that he's the only non-gay drag queen in London. I know a few in LA but – surely

not?

"Like a brother to me."

"Oh, great. Sorry, got to go. Drago needs walking."

Drago picked up his lead with a hopeful look on his face. "Just give me a minute, boy. I've got a bike to buy! Eleven grand to keep her brother sweet is well worth it!"

He whined and settled down at my feet, the lead in his mouth. A minute later, I pocketed my phone and walked out the door. It was surprising how quickly you could spend money. Drago looked slightly disappointed when I didn't break into a run the second we left the apartment. I looked down at his face and shrugged. "Sorry buddy, I've hurt my ankle and can't face pounding the streets."

He groaned and pulled on his lead. "Hang on, I've got an idea. Jump in the car and I'll take you to the park." I swear he smiled as he scrabbled into the front seat, peering out of the windscreen as though he was a king on a throne. Normally, he'd sit in the back, but the bike was taking up all the room.

Once we got to the park, I parked the car and opened the boot. With a shrug, I pulled out the bike and looked at Drago. "What do you think? Can you put up with the embarrassment of me riding a lady's bike with a pink rose on it for the sake of a decent walk?" By the look on his face, he wasn't fussed at all. I hopped onto the bike and pedalled off. God, I couldn't have ridden a bike for a long time, steering and pedalling seemed remarkably hard, as if I was being asked to pat my head and rub my stomach at the same time, and then it struck me that the handlebars weren't in line with the seat. My mind went back to when it thudded into the back of my seats, so I got off and wrestled them back into place. After that, cycling was a lot easier. Drago galloped off, pulling me along, his tongue lolling out of his mouth, pedalling with him beside me, I had a smile on my face so wide, I looked like Lightning McQueen and swallowed as many flies as he had collected leaves in his grill while cruising with Sally.

By the time I returned to the car, at least one photographer had taken a picture of me riding a lady's bicycle. It was a bit worrying that so many paparazzi spent their time hanging around a park on the off chance they'd spot a celebrity doing something newsworthy. I had to wonder what they did the rest of the time, and whether they ever got arrested for dodgy behaviour.

As soon as I got in, I fed Drago and headed for the shower. Rick was due any minute, and we were both travelling into the city for a radio interview promoting Guy Fawkes. I dressed smart casual and was combing my hair when the doorbell rang, and Rick entered.

"Good, you're all ready!" he said, breezing into the apartment like he had a thousand times before. "Drago," he greeted my dog, who immediately trotted up to him and accepted the treat Rick took out of his pocket.

"Thank God you don't come over here often," I said. "He would be as fat as a barrel if you did."

Drago looked up from his basket and huffed.

Rick grinned and pushed his hands into his pockets. "The poor thing would starve to death if he relied solely on you."

"Nonsense, he's an athlete, not a Roly Poly manager

who spends too much time eating out and sitting on his behind."

Rick looked down at the buttons of his shirt bulging at the seams and nodded, raising an eyebrow he replied, "Perhaps you're right, but some of us rely on brains rather than brawn in our lives, which brings me to the point of me coming here. There are reports you were seen in one of London's parks riding a lady's bike. Is that true?"

I sighed. "Really? That's doing the rounds already? I borrowed a friend's bike because I hurt my ankle and Drago needed a run." I narrowed my eyes. "Hang on, why did you come here for a 'chat'?"

He sat down on the sofa and picked up a game controller. I pursed my lips; this was his ploy for tackling a subject he knew would get my goat up. Do the old 'mates playing a video game' routine while he slipped in the fact that the purple shirt I wore on the chat show made me look bilious, or that I should smile more when I'm talking to a female interviewer; flirt and use my considerable charm. And when I'm talking to a male presenter to wink and throw in a few innuendos, so that I appeared approachable, as if I was one of the boys, not a posh twat - as Rick liked to put it.

I picked up the other controller and switched on the game console. Sitting down beside him, I asked. "Are you sure we have time for this? You can just come out with whatever nugget of wisdom you feel I should subscribe to, without softening me up with some buddy time, you know, Rick. I'm a big boy, I can take the criticism. If I couldn't, I wouldn't be doing this job."

"Ah, and there was me thinking you only did it to get

pussy and an Aston Martin?"

I slashed my sword through his opponent. "Do you think I need fame to get women?"

Rick respawned his character. "Probably not, but to maintain your heart throb image, it doesn't hurt to feather your nest with a beautiful woman or two. While in Hollywood, rumours had it you had a few romps with your co-star and there was talk of several other flings as well. But the only woman you've made the headlines with in the last fortnight is the Beast. It really wouldn't do your public persona any harm to mingle with a few beauties, or at least allude to it when you're doing interviews."

I hacked off his character's head and grinned grimly. "Rick, I'm nearly forty. For the last two decades, I've dated..." I waved my hands about. "A lot of women. More than I can think of. When I was younger, it was fun, exciting and thrilling, but over the last few years, well, I want more. I want someone I can come home to that has my back and with whom I can be myself. Perhaps, have a couple of kids to drive me up the wall. I want what my parents have - a partnership."

"I never said you can't have that, Tom. But let's face it, in two decades, have you ever got close to it? Some people aren't made for that type of commitment, and you, my friend, are one of those." He held up his hands. "Hey, I get it! If I looked like you, and was as successful, I probably wouldn't be happily married either. Why have one cookie when you can have the whole jar?"

"Bah!" I got off the sofa and switched off the console. Striding to the door, I said, "Fine, I'll do as you ask in public, but in private, things are going to change. I'm tired of the chase!"

CHAPTER 20

BETH

We never saw Susie for the rest of the week. After the argument with Hunter, she decided to stay with her boyfriend, James. She texted me and explained her blow up wasn't entirely because of Hunter cake shaming her. Apparently, work was stressing her out, and the curse made her want to bite anyone other than James's head off. Kind of the opposite from what a praying mantis would do, is how she put it, which, despite me being slightly waspish about her proclaiming I wouldn't have a chance with Tom until I was dead, made me laugh.

Come Saturday morning, I was really missing her, but I was fortunate to have Hunter rallying my corner and he was completely ecstatic with the new arrival of an impressively priced racing bike.

"He's a keeper!" he had proclaimed as he kissed the seat as though it were a long-lost lover.

"The man has lost his marbles," I said, eying the bike as though it was the crown jewels. "Eleven grand for a bike, for you. Absolutely frigging mental. He must have hit his head when he fell."

And then when we saw a newspaper clipping with

Tom riding the lady's silver bike around the park with Drago towing him, I bit my lip, and my heart leapt every time his name came up in social media or the television, convinced he'd been rushed into hospital with a life-threatening concussion. Hunter merely rolled his eyes and tutted at my concern.

"You daft bat, he's promoting his latest movie."

"There must be something wrong, Hunter," I said, gnawing on a fingernail.

"Oh, how have you worked that out, pray tell me?"

"Because he hasn't texted and told me it was all a mistake and that he won't be able to make it today."

"And why would he do that, huh?"

"You've seen the interviews and heard him on the radio. He's a ladies' man, and cavorting with a string of beauties, why would he waste a Saturday hanging out with me? This is so out of character for him. There must be an explanation for it? I hope he hasn't got a blood clot or anything like that."

Hunter sat on the sofa with a sigh. "This is all Susie's fault. If she hadn't been such a cynic and said the things she did to you, you wouldn't think it's odd that Tom wants to spend time with you. He likes you Beth, even if it's just in a friendly way, which, I don't think it is, he'd rather have an afternoon riding you than with all the leading ladies."

I snorted a laugh. "Not riding me, Hunter, you ass, horse riding!"

"Right, isn't that what I said?"

"No, you didn't." I sat down beside him and threaded my arm through his, leaning my head on his shoulder.

"I told you, Beth, you and I are going to get our man."

"Talking of which, has Liam asked you out yet?"

"Ah, no. Not exactly, but he took advantage of the time I got my hands caught in the sleeves of my outfit," he said, grinning.

"You're sleeping with him?" I asked, wide eyed.

"I wouldn't say sleeping, but we're doing everything else."

"Oh?" I frowned, unable to work out their relationship. "He hasn't asked you out yet?"

"No, but it's only a matter of time." He raised his eyebrows twice at me.

"I hope you're right, Hunter. I'd hate it if he's only using you for sex." I almost slapped myself. How many times had Susie and I sat here and said the exact same thing about some ex-boyfriend of Hunter's, who had been hammering on our door begging to see him? Some might say that what was happening between Hunter and Liam was karma. Although Hunter was always straight with his many exes that he wasn't in it for the long haul, few of them believed him.

"Oh, he's using me alright. You wouldn't believe what he made me do the other day. It was…"

I clapped a hand over his mouth. "Some things are better left a mystery, Hunter, such as what's in sausages and what happens when fifty thousand watts travel through the human body."

Hunter chuckled and looked at his watch. "Okay, enough about me and Liam. Now, you have three and a half hours before Tom picks you up, time to hit the shower and start your beautification. I'll make breakfast and don't say you can't eat anything because you know how travel sick you get if you're hungry. Go on, jump in the shower. Hop it!"

I got off the sofa and placed a kiss on his forehead. "Have I ever told you I love you?" I asked.

"Not nearly enough, lover girl."

He'd been working at the Trap Door the night before and on discovering I was awake at four, when he'd come in had kept me company ever since, talking about anything and everything to take my mind off the butterflies' salsa dancing in my insides. I hoped he'd catch a few z's after Tom picked me up, as dark shadows were already bruising his eyes. Although they didn't distract from his beauty, only gave him a vulnerable and ethereal look, which made me want to scoop him up in my arms and hold his heart to my breast.

"Chop, chop, bitch, and use my concealer. Your bags are bigger than mine!"

I smirked and disappeared into the bathroom.

Looking in the mirror, I rubbed a finger over my face. It was true a purple blush tainted the skin under my eyes, but on the whole my skin was my best feature, soft as a peach, clear, and fine with a rosy hue. Of course, I also had exceptional ear lobes that were hidden under my hair most of the time. I'm not sure, if polled, that many men would admit to dating their other half because their earlobes were awesome. Only a guess, but I've never heard of an ear man before. Shame, as I'd have a steady stream lining up outside my door if that were the case. Perhaps I should pull my hair back, put some gold studs in and let Tom have a sneak peek of my sexy lugholes and see if that had the desired effect?

I pulled my hair back into a ponytail, low enough to get a riding hat on, but showing a tantalising amount of lobe. Then dabbed on some concealer, a flash of mascara and slipped on jeans and a t-shirt. Perfect!

Now it was time for breakfast and a cup of tea. The aroma of coffee and eggs teased my nostrils into breathing deeply and padding into the main living area. Hunter stood behind the breakfast bar with a pair of jogging bottoms on and an apron in the shape of a French maid's outfit. I grinned, even though I hated the man for looking so good in something as ridiculous as that.

"Scrambled eggs and toast, plus a lovely cup of char. When are you going to do your makeup, Beth?"

I smiled. "Thanks for this," I said, taking the plate and cup over to the window and sitting at the small table. "And I've finished my face. See, no visible bags and we're only going horse riding, not out to some fancy restaurant."

Hunter sneered his lip. "It wouldn't hurt to make a little more effort."

"I have. I've got my ears on show. At least, some of them. Gold studs and all!" I said, flitting a hand up to cup the shell of my ear and push a little bit of hair back. "See?"

"Woo hoo! You've pushed the boat out this time. One flash of those sexy studs and the man's going to be on his knees." He rolled his eyes at me and huffed. "And that loose tee and shapeless jeans will have totally the right effect."

I raised my eyebrows. "I'm horse riding, and I need to be comfortable. The green and brown flatter me, don't you think so?"

"I think it's highly likely that the SAS, if they're about, will take you on instantly as a cadet. I just need to add a bit of camouflage to your face, and you'll blend in with the countryside perfectly."

My face crumpled as I pinched the t-shirt between my finger and thumb. "This isn't a good colour on me then?"

He slapped a hand to his forehead. "Eat that and then come with me and I'll tell you what to wear, Little Miss, I don't have a clue."

CHAPTER 21

TOM

Looking over at Jane sat in the seat of my Range Rover, I couldn't fail to notice the plunging V-necked tee in fuchsia, paired with black stretchy leggings. Although I wasn't complaining at the sight, I couldn't help but wonder if she'd remembered we were going riding today. Her hair pulled back in a ponytail sat around her shoulders, showing off gold studs, her eyes were pinned to where her hands were wedged between her knees.

"I love your earrings," I said, rolling my eyes at my comment. She reached up and brushed her fingers over her ears. "You remembered we're horse riding today, didn't you?" I asked.

Her head jerked up, and she looked at me as if someone had drowned her cat.

"This is a bad idea, isn't it? I won't be offended if you want to turn back," she said.

My gaze scanned the road ahead as my lips tightened into a thin line. "What on Earth gave you the idea I wanted to turn around?" My eyes flicked to her, and I noticed her cheeks colour. I sighed. "Ah Jane, don't do this." Her head jolted towards me as her mouth dropped open. I reached over and took her small hand from between her thighs and encased it in mine. "Don't hide from me, Jane. I wouldn't have asked you if I didn't want you to come. Are you nervous about getting on a horse? I promise I'll take care of you."

She licked her lips. "No, I'm not nervous about getting on a horse. I'm just wondering why you would invite me. I've been listening to your interviews on the telly and radio, and unless I'm mistaken, you have a lot of lady admirers. One being your latest co-star on the film you've just made, so why would you want to sit here with me?"

"Honestly Jane, I don't know why?" I said, gritting my teeth. "All I can say is that not everything you see or hear in an interview is true. There is always going to be a certain amount of spin to maintain the persona the public expects from someone with my reputation. I can't deny I've been a ladies' man over the years, and this might surprise you, but I have never had a one-night stand."

Her brow furrowed. "Really? Not one?"

I grinned. "No, not one. Unless you include my first time? I suppose technically that could be classed as a one-night stand. My Chemistry mistress when I was seventeen."

Jane's mouth dropped open. "Isn't that a real no, no? I mean teacher and student. You were seduced by an older woman in school?"

I nodded. "Ah ha, she made a man of me, and yes, she could have lost her career because of that one episode, but I wasn't going to say anything. When she wrestled me into the supply cupboard and pulled my trousers around my ankles, I had one thought in my mind."

She giggled. "What was that?"

"I'd ace chemistry."

She laughed out loud as my heart did a flip. "Did you?" she asked.

"Did I what?" I asked, glancing into her eyes and warming from the fire that burned within them.

"Did you ace chemistry?"

I smirked. "Ah ha did pretty well at biology too." She grabbed my thigh and gave it a squeeze, I jerked the wheel, and nearly put us in a ditch.

"Oh, sorry, I never meant to manhandle you like that," she said, removing her hand from my leg as though from a fire.

"It's alright, you can do it again any time you want. It just surprised me, that's all." I rubbed the place where her hand had sat, trying to rub the heat back to where her touch had scorched my flesh, leaving it cold and barren but my groin hot and tight. I shuffled in my seat, hoping she wouldn't notice the bulge and get the wrong idea. Somehow, I thought she'd spook if she realised how her touch had affected me.

"Well, here we are," I said, pulling into the entrance to my friend's home and travelling down an avenue of trees that eventually opened up into an impressive driveway. A massive water feature sat in front of the house, with prancing horses, spurting jets of water from their mouths. It loomed over the countryside, all stark limestone slabs and Georgian-style windows.

"Wow, he owns a Stately Home? Do we need to pay admittance, and will we get a tour of the grounds and finish up with a cream tea?"

I grinned, "I'm afraid not. This isn't some struggling estate needing the public to pay for the latest patches to its crumbling brickwork and leaking roof. It is in fact a new build, that's why it sticks out like a sore thumb. The owner is as rich as Croesus and eager for his rich and famous friends to frolic in his fortune. I think he gets bored since his retirement five years ago."

Jane sat forward in her seat and peered out the window. "Fancy." She smirked. "Will we see your friend today?"

"Doubtful, although you never know. He's probably on a yacht somewhere in the Pacific or mingling with a sheikh in his desert palace." I drove around the mansion to the rear of the property, where nestled in a wooded area out of view from the main house was a block of stables. I pulled up at a gate and watched as it swung open and Errol, the head groomsman, stepped out of a building on our left.

"Good morning, Tom, and this must be Jane? If you'd both come with me, I'll get you kitted out for your trek. Miss, if you follow me to the ladies' dressing room. I have some boots and a hat for you. Tom has been here enough times to sort himself out. And Tom, Excalibur's out in the yard waiting for you." Errol threw over his shoulder.

"Thanks. Have you sorted out a ride for Jane yet?"

"Yes, because I didn't know how experienced you were," he said, looking at Jane. "I've saddled up Misty. She's a nice calm ride. You shouldn't have any trouble with her."

"Thanks," Jane replied.

"Great," I said, giving her elbow a squeeze. "I'll meet you out in the yard in a minute."

"Have you ridden before, Jane?" Errol asked.

"Yes, but it was years ago. Hopefully, it will be like riding a bike. You know, it all comes flooding back to you after a shaky start."

***

Fifteen minutes later, Errol emerged with Jane in tow. She wore a hacking jacket and full-length riding boots. Apart from the daring fuchsia top, she looked the part. I held the reins of Excalibur as he chomped down on his bit enthusiastically and pawed the ground with his hoof.

Jane's gazed flitted up to mine and her mouth dropped open.

"Well, Rochester, you're only missing a big black cape and you'd look like the master."

Errol leaned over to Jane and whispered in her ear. She smirked and looked around for her mount. A look passed between us as I scraped my foot on the yard, mimicking Excalibur's. It seemed that Errol and Jane had already formed an alliance. I frowned and growled at him, "What's happened to Misty?"

The smile on Errol's face disappeared, and he called over to a stable lad asking him where Misty was.

"Oh sorry, Mr Wakeman, a lady came by and insisted she take Misty out. She said that Mr Austin's friend was an accomplished rider and would be happier on Zephyr."

I watched as the lad bought out a magnificent flea-bitten grey mare, the perfect contrast to Excalibur's midnight coat. Errol took a step forward and shook his head.

"I don't think that's a good idea. Zephyr's not suitable for a novice rider. Go saddle Chocolate instead."

The lad shifted from foot to foot. "I'm sorry he's already gone out."

Errol ground his teeth. "I thought I was in charge of these stables! Who allowed this change?"

The lad looked hopelessly around him. "The boss did, Mr Wakeman, he came in the yard just before Mr Austin with a couple of friends. I'm so sorry I didn't know what else to do."

Errol pursed his lips together. "Alright, I'll deal with this." He turned to me and said, "I'm terribly sorry sir, but I can only apologise. Zephyr isn't a suitable ride for Miss Jane, and I can only recommend you wait until the party returns and you can go out with Misty instead."

I looked over at Jane, who, after an initial hesitation, now stood leant up against Zephyr's massive shoulder and was running her hands down her mare's face. Jane's expression made me pause and grit my teeth. The mare had lowered her head, letting it docilely bob at each touch. "Bloody horse whisperer," I muttered. "Why can't she lay her hands on me like that?" But as her gaze met mine, all the fire left me, and my lips turned up as though

I was a simpleton. "Jane, what would you like to do?" I asked.

She bit her lip and then glanced at the horse. "She's beautiful. Big as a house, but I'm sure with your help, and taking it easy, we could have an enjoyable time riding."

Oh, how I wished she was talking about something else.

"There, that's settled Errol. Between the two of us, we'll take care of it."

Errol frowned. "You realise Zephyr will want to match Excalibur and he'll do his utmost to show off in front of her?"

I looked over at Jane and the passive Zephyr and nodded. "Don't worry, we've got this."

The decision made; Jane looked nervously at the saddle. "She's enormous," she said.

I walked over and touched her arm. Her slight frame trembled under my touch. "Just put your foot in the stirrup and swing your leg over." I dipped under the reins and pulled on the opposite stirrup as Jane mounted. In a movement, I'm not sure I've ever seen another human make before. She hopped up and down on her leg a few times and then half scrambled up onto the saddle and gave us all a bewildered look, before losing her balance and flopping forward over her mount's rump. Pushing her fingers up towards the saddle, she sat up and grinned.

I half expected the mare to bolt or at least prance about under this unexpected and odd sensation, but she didn't bat an eyelid.

"Er, Miss, you're the wrong way around," Errol said,

rubbing at his skull.

"Yes, so I am." Jane flushed scarlet and executed an around the world as though she'd done it a million times before. Facing the right way, she took up the reins and looked down at her cleavage brimming from the edges of her sexy top. "Ugh," she said, yanking the top upwards and pulling the two edges of her hacking jacket together. "Sorry, it's been a while since I've ridden."

Why that statement made a bulge appear in my jodhpurs, I wasn't sure. Probably an eyeful of Jane's breasts didn't help, but it made me briefly wish I'd left my jeans on.

Stunned, Errol and I silently adjusted the stirrup lengths and tightened the girth. I lingered a few moments more, hoping my arousal would dwindle when Jane's horse jerked forward and bolted out of the yard at a gallop.

"Tom!" Errol shouted as he lurched for Excalibur's reins, as the horse skittered, preparing to follow the mare.

In a panic, I leapt onto his back, hitting myself hard in a rather delicate part of my anatomy, and galloped after her. My heart was pounding so hard in my chest I barely noticed the pounding in another part of me until I spotted Jane beside a copse of trees, sedately waiting for me to catch up. As we approached, Zephyr pulled at her reins and lowered her head to munch on the grass. I guessed she was playing it cool as Excalibur pranced forward in a bouncy trot, which only made things worse. I hopped off and stood behind my stallion, trying to hide how much pain I was in.

Jane swung her leg over the saddle and hurriedly

made her way to me.

"Tom, are you hurt? You look dreadfully pale?"

"Yes, yes, just winded myself in my rush to follow you." I leaned into Excalibur, bringing my knees together and bending, my face flushed.

She made her way around my mount and took hold of my shoulders, running a hand through my hair. "Are you sure you're alright? You look feverish now."

"It will pass," I growled. "I thought you were going to get killed when the damn horse bolted!"

"Yes, that was a tad unexpected. My fault I'm afraid. In my excitement, I kicked her, and she went with it. I completely forgot about the acceleration on these things." She patted her mare, who had followed her around and was now face to face with Excalibur. "Tom, did you hit yourself on the pommel?"

"So hard my balls shot into my throat for a second," I said.

She chuckled and turned me to face her. "You poor man, would you like me to rub them better?" She clapped a hand over her mouth.

"Don't make me laugh!" I grimaced, smiling. "And if I wasn't so sore right now, the answer would be an emphatic yes." I winked.

"Would anything help?"

"Yes, an ice pack, but I don't suppose you have one of those on you?"

"Alas no. I'm hopeless at getting organised. No brownie points for me, I'm afraid."

I moved a little closer to Jane and ran my finger around her face, where a stray strand of hair floated across her nose. I took hold of it and tucked it under her hat. She leaned into me, the reins still in her hand, her other caressing my lower back. The top of her head only coming to my chest. I pulled her to me and hugged her into my body. For a moment, she went rigid, and I thought she would turn away. Then she dropped the reins and encircled my waist, careful not to bump into my groin. She softened into my body until I could feel every inch. Like a tonic, a wave washed through me and the only thing I could feel was her heart beating in rhythm with mine.

CHAPTER 22

BETH

After a while, Zephyr nudged me in the back and broke the spell. I stepped away from Tom and smiled.

"Would you like to go back to the stables now, sir?" I asked.

Tom blinked and gave himself a little shake. "What? No, let's go for our ride."

"Are you sure you're up to it?"

"Well, I'm not sure if I'm up to all sorts of riding, but I think I can manage a trot around the field."

I tutted and threw him a look.

"What? Weren't you offering a roll in the hay?" he asked. Getting back on his horse.

"You may be used to that from your usual company, but no, this filly wasn't offering that! Come on, Mr Rochester, show me how you control that magnificent beast between your legs before my mare succumbs to his charms and there's a whole lot of different mounting going on."

Zephyr snorted down Excalibur's nostrils a few times, she then backed into him and flicked her tail in his face. I hopped on with a lot more grace than the first time and kicked her into action.

"What's wrong with your mare succumbing to this stallion's attentions?" Tom asked as he raced after me.

I dug my heels in as Zephyr streaked across the field like a lightning bolt. Excalibur thundered after us like the devil at our heels, his nostrils flaring wide as his hooves tore up the grass. We raced into some woods and weaved our way through the trees until another group of riders caught my attention ahead and I eased Zephyr into a trot. Excalibur, hot on our heels, shot into the back of us as my mare danced about daintily. I patted her neck to calm her down.

"I thought you were a novice!" Tom said, wrestling an over excited Excalibur.

"I never said I was a novice, only that I hadn't ridden for a long time. When I was younger, I more or less lived and breathed the local stables. A typical teenage girl more interested in horses than boys."

"When did that change?" Tom asked as we walked our mounts towards the group.

The ground here, saturated with standing water, clung to our horses' hooves and glooped at each step. I raised my head and surveyed the group in front of us. There were five riders, three men and two women partially hidden behind the leaders.

"John," Tom called, "when did you get back to England? I thought you were on a yacht somewhere in the middle of the ocean?"

"I was until yesterday. I arrived earlier this morning

by helicopter. I'm afraid we took your mount. Leigh's too nervous to ride Zephyr, it looks as if your friend's mastered her though." He squinted his piercing black eyes at me, and I shifted under his gaze. I had the uncanny sensation he'd stripped me bare, right down to my bones.

A loud bang echoed through the trees, unnerving the horses. One of them shot forward and after colliding with Zephyr and the black wall that Excalibur presented slashed out with its hindquarters, booting my mare's rump and setting her swerving violently to one side. She and I parted ways as her back legs dropped away and she scrambled to get to her feet, dumping me unceremoniously into a swampy quagmire as she righted herself. I landed with a splash and curled up in a ball until the frightened horses settled down.

As I cleared the mud from my face. Mr Rochester glowering down on me with eyes as dark and turbulent as water flooding a ravine.

"Blast it, Jane, get to your feet before you're trampled upon," he said, snatching up Zephyr's reins and leading her towards me. "Get on. We're leaving!"

My shoulders drooped. I took hold of the reins and dragged myself back into the saddle, squelching as I found my seat. My heart thundered in my chest and hot tears burned at the back of my eyes. Not because I was physically hurt, or my pride dented, but the look on Tom's face cut the deepest.

Anger rolled off him in waves, his face as immoveable as a mountain. Red faced with an aching heart, I slouched in my saddle and followed him as he rode in silence back to the stable yard.

Errol's mouth dropped open the minute he spotted us. He rushed forward and grabbed Zephyr's bridle.

"Did she throw you Miss?" he asked.

"No, not really. A shot went off, and another horse collided with her. She stumbled, and we parted ways. Really, it wasn't anyone's fault."

"Yes, it bloody was!" Tom threw over his shoulder.

I swallowed hard as a black cloud enveloped me. Zephyr dropped her head, and we plodded on.

The sound of a horse galloping towards us had Tom swinging around in his saddle. Any moment, I thought he'd draw a sword from his back and run it through the next person he came across.

"What the blazes do you want?" he thundered.

"I'm so sorry. Jane, are you hurt?" The owner of this fine estate and those perceptive black eyes said. "Tom, you have to understand it was purely an accident."

Tom swung his legs over Excalibur's back and marched over to his friend, looking as though he would pull him from his horse and beat him into a bloody pulp.

"Do you usually have riflemen on your grounds, John?"

Errol stepped forward, a frown on his brow. John shook his head and looked over at his head stableman.

"No one shoots on this land. John, I promise you I would know if someone was firing a gun."

"Then what was that blasted noise, Errol? Tell me that! Why hasn't security informed me?"

"Who do you think caused that pandemonium out there?" Tom asked. "That bloody witch, that's who!"

"Tom?" John asked.

"Alisha my ex, who else?"

I slipped off Zephyr and led her closer to the men, a crinkle between my eyes.

"Alisha, there isn't an Alisha in my party, Tom."

"I believe you called her Leigh, but it was that witch alright. She had her phone in her hand. I bet it was her that set off that gunshot sound in her mount's ear and damn near killed Jane in the process!"

I could have wept with relief. He wasn't angry with me after all, only concerned for my safety.

"But why would she do that Tom, when your relationship ended months ago, or didn't it?"

"Yes, but since then, she's had it in for Jane. It was her that sent the pictures of Jane looking a wreck after I knocked her off her bike." Tom explained.

I straightened my shoulders and brushed my hands down my sodden brown stained top, trying not to expose too much bosom.

"Jane's the beast?" John asked, shaking his head and then looking at me with mud dripping down my face and grinning. "Okay, I can see it now. Sorry sweetheart, but you look a mess. Go and take a shower in the ladies, wash that crap off and change. Errol, make sure she has some dry clothes to wear."

"Yes, boss."

"Charlie, take the horses and brush them down. Tom, you'd better come with me. I'm not about to fall out with you over some ex-bimbo who's taken a dislike to…". I could hear the mirth in his words. "The beast. Some second-rate actress who believes she's the next Sandra Bullock. I guess that's why she wanted Misty, just to see Jane come a cropper."

"Hold on a minute, Jane!" Tom called to my back. I turned and watched him striding towards me. Holding my arm, he peered into my face. "I didn't ask you if you were alright. I'm sorry that should have been my first concern. Well, it was when I saw you rolled up in the mud like a champion jockey, but then I saw Alisha and my world turned red."

I blinked, hoping the mud obscured the tears in my eyes. "It's fine, I'm good, no harm done." I croaked.

"I'll see you in a minute. I just need to have a word with the enormous *ass* who let Alisha snatch your ride and send you into the mud."

Looking over at Tom's friend, a man as rich as Croesus, who should by all rights be as old as the hills. But, in fact, was vital and provoking and who, it seemed, didn't mind being referred to as an ass. I watched his gaze intensify as he watched us as keenly as a hawk viewing its prey, as a shiver coursed down my spine.

I gave Tom a smile resembling Stephen King's Carrie with blood dripping over her skull – of course, mine was ditch water and faecal matter - and I turned to follow Errol into the changing block.

"It looks as though you've made quite an impression on both men, Miss. Intriguing," said Errol. "Showers are over there. Towels and shampoo are as you walk in. Do you have a change of clothing with you?" he asked, gesturing to my sports bag sat next to a rack where I'd changed into the riding boots.

"Yes, I'm not sure about underwear, though. I never expected I'd change that after my ride. Not that I'd expect you to have any I could borrow."

My brows wrinkled as I took in the other vanity cases and assembled footwear.

"You don't need to worry... Jane, isn't it? Security has escorted Alisha to the gates. I will send her change of clothes to her later today."

"Oh, thank you. And my name's Beth. Jane is kind of a... nickname Tom calls me. It's actually my middle name." I sat down on the bench and fiddled with the slippery leather as I tried to pull my boots off. Errol knelt in front of me and grabbed the heel of my boot, helping me release my foot. "How come you've had Alisha escorted from the property? I mean, I was there, and I never realised that one of the party was her, or that she caused the sound that startled the horses?"

"Mr St John is very strict on security. A man of his wealth has to be. I'm surprised she got on the estate in the first place. Although it's not common knowledge that Alisha was the leak in the news article involving Mr Austin and yourself." He shrugged.

"You just called your boss Mr St John. I thought his Christian name was John, isn't that so?"

"His friends call him John, but his real name is Rivers St. John. A bit like you, he has little choice in what people call him. To be fair, most people find Rivers an unlikely first name."

"I like it. It suits him better than John. John is so mundane and ordinary whereas Rivers is…?" I rolled my eyes around the room, trying to find the right word to describe Errol's master. "Enigmatic."

Errol chuckled. "He's a good boss; fair but rigid and demanding. I wouldn't want to work for anyone else. Perhaps a little unorthodox, but a man in his position has a right to be a little eccentric. He's also an excellent judge of character."

He released my second boot. Gathering them, he rose to his feet and made his way to the exit.

"Errol! Before you go, why did you tell me all that about Mr St John?"

He turned and considered my face for several seconds before answering. "It's unusual for both men to find a woman – interesting."

I watched him retreat, a frown etched into my brow. After a minute, I shook my head and went to have a shower.

CHAPTER 23

TOM

My gaze never left Jane's until she had disappeared completely. I turned back to John and noticed a sardonic smile danced around his lips.

"What are you doing with a woman like her?" he asked.

"We're friends, John."

"Is that all you are?"

"Yes. No, why do you care what she is to me?"

"She's piqued my curiosity, or rather, you have. She's not your usual type, is she?"

"And what is my usual type, John?"

"Superficially beautiful and as solid as cotton candy. So why turn your attention to Jane, the beast to your beauty?"

I ground my teeth together. What was wrong with John today? He rarely showed much interest in who I dated; he was always the polite spectator. "Jane isn't a beast, Rivers."

"No, but she's hardly striking, either." His lips turned

up mockingly. "Unless you're into the swamp thing from the black lagoon?"

"Pfft, still an ass St John! Jane's attractive, just in an understated way. But she's fun, caring and surprising."

"A curio then? Like one of those Trolls or a Cabbage Patch doll?"

"Why are you poking sticks at me, John? Jane and I are none of your business."

"You have to admit, it's a surprising thing, you turn up here with an ordinary woman, ready to smash anyone's face in who mistreats her, and then there's the matter of using every inch of my name in the last five minutes. What's happened to just John? God, I haven't heard you call me Rivers since the first day at school!"

"Jane isn't just an ordinary woman. If you think that you're as blind as I was. I don't know why I ever started calling you John. It doesn't suit your conniving nature."

"And Tom doesn't suit you either. All that dark brooding and moodiness. What does she call you? I believe Errol heard the name Rochester?"

"So, you have Errol spying for you now?"

"He wears a com and earpiece, Tom. It's a security measure. And don't think I'm blind to what Jane has to offer. I, unlike you, have often dated women for something other than the way they look."

"Wonderful! Now you're calling me shallow." I turned and strode away from him.

He took hold of my arm. "Wait Tom, we've been friends for years. I'm not your enemy here. I just want to know if you're serious about this girl?"

I shook off his grip and turned to face him. "Why, what does it matter to you how I feel about her?"

He didn't answer. My eyes narrowed. "Oh, come on! You've met her once! You've always been interested in my castoffs."

He laughed derisively. "Two, out of the many you've left in your wake. Both serious relationships – one I married."

I watched as sadness filled his eyes and turned away under his crushing grief, kicking myself, despite a pang of jealousy creeping into my heart. "I want what you and Lucy had." I admitted.

"And you think you can have it with her?"

I faced him, looking at his expression filled with brotherly concern. "I don't know, but I want to give it a try. If she'll have me?"

He nodded. "Come by the house before you leave and have some lunch with me. My other guests aren't staying."

"Sure, as long as you don't get any ideas about Jane. I don't relish the prospect of vying for her attentions with you."

"She's not interested in wealth."

"No, but she would be in the man behind it. He's an incorrigible charmer."

His lips picked up at the corners and he walked back to the house, hands in his pockets, whistling as he went.

***

I showered and changed quickly and exited the changing rooms to find Jane hanging over a stable door, smiling as she chatted with Errol. She'd pulled her hair back into a glossy brown ponytail and wore jeans with a green and brown top that complimented her colouring. It made the pink rose of her lips and the soft blush of her cheeks pop. I found myself grinning as she stroked Zephyr's nose while Errol brushed the mare down.

She looked over her shoulder and grinned at me. Zephyr's soft muzzle nudged her, eager for attention, and I imagined I was the horse having her hands roam over me. I stopped myself before my mind went in a direction that would only make my jeans tighten so much, I'd find it hard not to push her into a stable and behave like Excalibur would, given the chance with Zephyr.

"John invited us up to the house for lunch. Are you happy to go?" I asked.

Jane raised her eyebrows. "You two put your differences behind you? Because I really don't want to be in the middle of the pair of you clashing horns."

Horn. Why did she have to mention that word? I was straight back in the stable again, thinking just what I would do with my horn given the chance. Perhaps it was better to stay here and have John cool my ardour than have Jane to myself and be tempted to stop off somewhere on the way home and convince her to sleep over?

"Harmless banter. John and I have known each other for years. He's like a brother to me." Always there to knock me down to size and stop me getting too big for my boots, I failed to add.

"Another brother? You have so many already, it's hardly fair." She grinned and nudged my shoulder. "Yes then, let's stay. I'd like to get to know Rivers better. He seems an interesting man." I scowled as she looped her arm around mine. "And much younger and more attractive than I expected."

"Well, I wouldn't go that far."

"Of course, nowhere near as interesting as you," she said.

I raised my eyebrows at her, and she grinned. "Or?" I prompted.

"Or what?"

I pointed at myself, gesturing to my finer features.

She opened her eyes wide. "Oh, yes. Not as attractive as you are. Although I've only seen him from a distance, and those piercing black eyes..." She shivered. "Compelling, I hardly noticed anything else. Certainly not his strong shoulders, firm chin and the dazzle of his white teeth."

"You're teasing me, Jane?" I said, turning her to face me.

She smiled, reached up, and kissed my cheek. "Dear Mr Rochester," she sighed and walked us towards the house. "Did I mention his chest?" she asked.

"What about his chest?" I growled.

Her laughter tinkled. "Not nearly as impressive as yours."

"As long as we're clear, I possess something better than him."

She squeezed my arm, and I grinned until I spotted John watching our approach. I wished I'd driven the car and driven straight out the gates. For a moment, I considered swinging Jane around to face me and stamping my mark on her, so there was no doubt who she belonged with.

CHAPTER 24

BETH

I looked about me as we entered Rivers' home. My mouth dropped open at the grandeur of the place. A staircase dominated the space as it swept up to the second story and parted in the centre, flowing around to embrace a massive wraparound landing. It was overlooked by a huge stained-glass window, that cast a radiant light that danced warmly on the rich dark oak treads. The largest Persian silk rug I'd ever seen in my life laid at its feet on a marble chequerboard floor. I pushed the toe of my converse trainers into the pile, alive with the colours of a molten sunset of red, orange and indigos.

It was a fascinating mixture of old and new, classic and contemporary, and as the man himself stepped into the room. I had no doubt it suited him perfectly. Dressed in black jeans and a pure white shirt, which enhanced his black eyes and midnight hair, streaked through with a smattering of grey, he looked youthful and yet mature at the same time.

A smile stretched across his face, making his eyes sparkle as if they were pools of liquid jet. I took a breath and released my hold on Tom's arm.

"Tom. Jane, welcome to my home, won't you please

follow me into the lounge? I've had a light lunch laid out for us in the orangery. It's a much less formal space and one of mine, and the children's favourite spaces in the entire house." He took hold of my arm and guided me through a lounge with comfortable cream sofas, a large television, lemon damask wallpaper, and a warm wood floor. Beautiful rosewood and mahogany furniture sat laden with silver photo frames adorning it, the smiling faces of an attractive blonde woman and two giggling children shone from the tasteful family pictures. I caught a glimpse of one showing Rivers and his family altogether, their hair wet and tussled by a sea breeze, looking excited and happy, possibly from a foreign holiday. Along with the knickknacks on the sideboard, where an assortment of children's paraphernalia; an action figure, a game controller, and a small brown bear. "I have two children, Jane, a boy and a girl. They're at school now, but I'll pick them up in a few hours. Since their mother's death, I like to be there when they finish school, and I'm lucky enough to be able to do that most days."

I glanced behind at Tom, strolling along with a scowl on his face, and gave him a warm smile.

"I'm so sorry to hear of the loss of your wife. Are your children still very young, Rivers?"

"Cassie's the baby at nine and Jahan's eleven. Too young to be without their mother, but unfortunately, we are only pawns to be played, as fate wills us. Lucy died eighteen months ago in a car accident, Beth. It's been hard on all of us, but I was fortunately blessed to have a very happy marriage." He shrugged. "Come, enough sad talk. The orangery is not only a wonderful place to sit and eat, it also has some fabulous specimens I'd like to show you and some great hiding places. Not that I'm suggesting you hide away, merely that the children's favourite game is to hide and then spring out unexpectedly and frighten the pants off one." He smirked apologetically. "Listen to me. I've spent too long playing with my children."

"Well, I think that's a very admirable thing to do, Rivers. I'm sure your children love every minute you spend with them. Tell me, how did you come to name your son Jahan? I don't think I've ever heard that before."

"Lucy named him that, as a nod to my Persian ancestry. Jahan means world. Lucy always said he meant the world to her. Of course, when Cassie came along, it was my turn to choose the name. Not nearly as poetic as my wife. I called her Cassie because I liked the name and for no other reason." He chuckled and led us into a verdant paradise infused with an abundance of tropical flora.

"Wow, this is wonderful, Rivers. An escape from the everyday into something amazing and magical."

"I'm glad you like it, Beth. Somehow, I knew you'd appreciate it. I knew it from the first time I saw you."

"Perceptive aren't you, John?" Tom said from behind us.

Rivers looked behind him and his lip curled. "I like to think I'm a good judge of character, yes. That's why we've been friends so long."

"Friends, is that what you'd call us?

"Yes, I would, and I hope Beth can be a friend too?"

"I'd like that Rivers, very much," I said, Watching

Tom's expression keenly. I noticed a dark cloud fall over his face, and I took hold of his hand and linked his fingers through mine.

"Why don't you show Beth some of my orchids, Tom? Would you both like tea?"

We nodded as Rivers left the room.

"You like him, don't you Jane?"

"Yes, very much," I said.

"Huh, I didn't think wealth impressed you?"

"It doesn't particularly, but you can't help gasp at his home, it huge but highly individual and yet, it remains a family home. All those little personal touches dotted around are delightful. He's such a charming man and very gracious to welcome a nobody like me into his home."

"You're not a nobody, you're with me."

"Well, aren't I the fortunate one then?" I teased, grabbing onto his elbow.

"Hmph, that's not what I meant," he said, leading us through a winding pathway between the foliage.

I grinned up into his face. "I know you didn't, Rochester. That doesn't mean I don't enjoy teasing you."

"Tormenting more like. Pretending you like Rivers more than me."

"Oh, I wasn't pretending. Since you walked into his house, you've been acting like a bear with a sore head."

"That's ridiculous Jane, we're friends, and why does he keep referring to you as Beth?"

"Precisely, and he keeps calling me Beth, because

that is my name, Rochester."

"Beth? That doesn't ring any bells."

"No, I don't suppose it would. You were drunk last time you heard it."

"Oh." We walked on in silence for a while and then he said, "I don't drink very often." He looked at me, his brows drawn together. "So, do you mind me calling you Jane?"

"Do you mind me calling you Rochester?" I replied.

"Tea's ready!" Rivers called from the area near the entrance of the orangery, where a round table and four chairs were set up.

"No Jane, I don't mind you calling me that at all. I actually quite like it."

"Good, because I'm happy to be your Jane." I smiled up at him and watched as his features softened and his mouth widened into an enormous grin.

"Follow me dear Jane, I'll guide you out of this jungle and safely back to the lunch table."

"Why, thank you, kind sir, I'm happy to be led by you." I reached up onto my tiptoes and placed a chaste kiss on his cheek.

"Since you like me so much, you could kiss me here," he said, pointing to his lips.

I lowered my head so he wouldn't see the flush on my cheeks and released my hold on his arm so he wouldn't notice the tremble of my fingers at the thought of touching him in that way. Pushing through the foliage, I grinned at Rivers playing mum as he poured out tea for us.

"Now, that's a pleasant sight," I said.

"You like to see a man domesticated, Beth?"

"I'm not averse to it, Rivers." I took a seat and spied a look at Tom through my lashes. A shiver coursed through me as I spotted his eyes boring into my face.

Rivers picking up on the tension, handed me a cup and said, "Sit down Austin. You towering over us, is making us feel like a couple of kids on the naughty step." Turning to me, he said, "I hope you like your tea strong, Beth? I'm incapable of making dishwater."

"My Dad brought me up on builder's tea. If you can't stand your spoon up in it, it's not strong enough."

"I've made salad. Are salmon and prawns alright for you? I know how this one needs to watch his diet." Rivers tapped Tom's stomach and smirked.

"Do you want to lift your shirt and compare tone?" Tom asked in a low growl.

"No thanks. I, unlike you, don't need to get my kit off because I'm playing some superhero. And I have no one to impress with my physique these days. As long as I can chase the children around and ride my horses, I'm happy."

My gaze travelled down Rivers' chest to his lean stomach, and I wondered whether there was a sixpack nestled under his shirt or whether he was just in great shape. He certainly didn't show any sign of middle-aged spread.

Tom lifted an eyebrow but didn't answer, instead he helped himself to some salad and pretended the conversation never took place.

"It looks delicious. Do you often cook for you and the children, or do you have a cook?"

"Day to day I usually cook, but if I hold a dinner party, then no, I leave it to the professionals. But I have to say, that is where my domestic skills end. So, how long have you known Tom? Are you an actor too?"

CHAPTER 25

TOM

Driving back from Rivers's, I kept my eyes on the road as the rain had swept in and made the road slick. A fine mist crept through the hedgerow and carpeted the surface with a smoky film that obscured the white lines and forced me to concentrate on where I was going, instead of where I wanted to look. Jane sat so silently beside me, watching the wipers sweep over the screen that I thought she had dozed off, when suddenly, she said, "Thank you for today, Tom. It was lovely to meet one of your friends and get to know you a bit better."

"Hem, I'm not so sure it was a good idea. I think he made quite an impression on you."

"I think a man like him would make an impression on anyone. He's like a living fire; all warmth and pent-up energy. Do you think he's lonely in that massive house on his own?"

"He has his children, and the house never seems to be free of guests. Of course, it's a big estate, and that alone keeps him busy."

"Yes, I'm sure he's a very busy man, perhaps too busy? And there's a lingering sadness about the place. I suppose that's to be expected. But he's still a young man. Do you think he'll ever marry again?"

I huffed. "Probably, we're the same age."

"To lose your wife like that, such a shame. His children are fantastic, though. I'm sure they're a great comfort to him."

"Yes, you were excellent with Cassie and Jahan."

"I thought they were adorable."

"Just like their father?" I replied, unable to keep the sourness out of my voice.

Jane turned her face towards mine. I watched from the corner of my eye as her eyes glittered in the darkness. I saw her mouth part and her tongue poke out to moisten her lips. Holding my breath, I waited for her to say something.

In the end, I couldn't help asking. "Can we stop talking about St. John now?"

"Yes Rochester, what would you like to talk about instead?"

I screwed up my face and thought. "Who was it who suggested you wear the fuchsia top?"

I flicked my gaze to hers as a grin pulled at her mouth. "Hunter, he said the green and brown one would have me signed up for the army in minutes."

"So, he approves of us?" I said, taking a firmer grip on the wheel.

"Certainly, our friendship."

"Is that what this is, friendship?" I glanced at the

road sign and scowled.

"I always thought we were friends, Tom. Didn't you?"

"Well, yes, but not only that. You don't think a man spends eleven grand, replacing a bike that's worth a few hundred because he just wants friendship, do you?"

"Oh, so you thought you could buy me then? Don't you realise a girl like me wouldn't need paying to date or sleep with you? She'd be too grateful, wouldn't she? Of course, that's ridiculous, because why would a Hollywood A-lister like you want to pursue a relationship with someone like me?"

"Hell Jane! That's not what I meant. I don't see you as a desperate woman who would clamour for any morsel of affection I'd show you. Why wouldn't I want to go out with a woman like you?" I pulled over on the side of the road and turned in my seat.

"Look at me Tom," she said, gesturing to herself. "I'm plain! Why have me, when you can, date one of the most beautiful women in the world? Why do you think you called me Jane in the first place? It was because I blended into the background."

"You never did that. You started calling me Mr Rochester and who else would you be other than Jane? Our relationship didn't start because of how we looked."

"It did for me, Tom. I took one look at you and couldn't believe I was lucky enough to work with this star who shone brighter than anyone else. You know that first day I saw you in the flesh, I really hoped to find fault, just so it would bring you down to my level. Oh, not totally, but a little more within my reach. From the first time I saw you on the big screen, I thought you were the handsomest man I'd ever set eyes on. Can you say the same about when you met me?"

"It's not just about looks, Jane. You and I connected. We complement each other, Ying and yang and all that."

"Or Beauty and the Beast?"

"A lot of beasts are breath-taking."

She wriggled in her seat. "That's not me though, is it?"

I reached across, wrapping my hand around the base of her skull, and drew her nearer. I could feel her hesitation and the urge to pull back, but I wasn't letting her get away with it. It was time to show her how serious I was about us, not just being friends. Mere inches apart, Jane clapped her hand over my mouth and said, "Stop, Tom. I am sorry, I just can't."

"Why the hell not?" I jerked back in my seat and looked at her as if she'd sprayed me with acid.

"I can't, not after Rivers…"

"Rivers? Damn Rivers to hell!"

I pulled the car back onto the road, spraying up a cloud of grit in my wake. The wheels slid on the wet surface and the back end snaked before it found traction. We drove the rest of the way home in silence. I pulled up in front of Jane's apartment block and scowled at the people passing by. She unclipped her seat belt and turned in her seat.

"Dear Mr Rochester. I had a lovely time with you

today. You misunderstood my reluctance for rejection, and that wasn't the case at all. It was the prawns that foiled us this time. I'm allergic to shellfish but thank you all the same." She gathered all her stuff together as her words sunk in.

"It wasn't because of John?"

"Only so much as he served them. If I knew you intended to kiss me, I would have warned you earlier. I wouldn't have wanted to have missed it. But I can't risk ending the day like a puffer fish. That would have been the final straw for my fragile ego. Goodnight Tom, sweet dreams."

I groaned as she closed the door. "You ass," I said to myself, hitting the wheel with the heel of my hand. After a moment's hesitation, I jumped out of my seat and ran after her. "Jane, wait!"

She swung around and watched me run towards her, one hand on the door. "Tom?" she said, with a Mona Lisa smile.

"I'm sorry, I've been an ass. Forgive me?"

"Yes, you have. It's one of the things I like about you."

"Me being an ass?" I asked, wanting to kiss her again.

She rolled her eyes at me and grinned. "No, not that. That you can admit when you've made a mistake. It's very endearing." She cupped my face with her hand and gave me a wink. "Maybe next time?"

I grinned, nodding, and had a hard job not to kick up my heels and cry. Then I walked back to the car. I didn't even mind when a traffic warden was there to greet me.

"You realise you've parked on a double yellow line, sir?" he said.

"Yep, it was worth it."

"That remains to be seen. Just because you're rich and famous doesn't make you above the law. You'll get a fine the same as everybody else. It's just a shame yours won't be higher, in my humble opinion, sir. You famous people have a responsibility to behave better than the masses. Lead the way. Not flout the rules."

"Ah ha, I deserve to be flogged and clapped in irons." I agreed.

"Er, I wouldn't go that far, sir. Not even I am that much of a barbarian." He narrowed his gaze. "I believe I've seen you in that position before."

"What, getting a ticket?"

"No, flogged and clapped in chains." He finished writing the ticket with a flourish, then added. "Like that sort of thing, do you?" My mouth dropped open. "Whatever floats your boat, sir. Although if you meant getting a ticket, I'd have to say your mother should be ashamed of you! Law breaker!" He handed it to me with a face screwed up like a prune.

"Don't you want an autograph?" Someone shouted from an upstairs window. I looked up and saw Hunter hanging out of the window. He had a dress on, and half his makeup done. Jane was beside him, grinning.

"No, I most certainly don't!" said the traffic warden. "Obviously, a friend of yours. I suppose this is normal for you. You artistic types are all the same... kinky weirdoes. Good day, sir."

"It's make believe," I said.

The warden looked back up to where Hunter was waving and blowing kisses out of the window. "If he won't, I will!" he called out.

I smirked and looked at the ticket. "One hundred and thirty quid?"

"Just remember to pay it at the end of the month."

I narrowed my eyes. "Doesn't that make it more expensive?" I asked his retreating figure as he strolled away.

"Better still, the month after that," was his parting comment.

CHAPTER 26

BETH

Hunter turned from the open window, grinning at me like the Joker from Batman. He closed it and stood with his hands on his hips, a twinkle in his eyes. "Well?" he asked.

"You've smudged your lipstick. Would you like me to reapply it for you?" I looked at the lips left on the glass and my heart dipped. Tom Austin, aka Edward Rochester, tried to kiss me! Woo Hoo! I suddenly believed in unicorns, water turning into wine, the fountain of youth, David slaying Goliath, and in my case, Tom and Beth sitting in a tree K I S S I N G! Who would think such miracles existed in the world? Not that it had actually happened, not yet. But it was sure to, going by how angry he was at my refusal. Ah, I wondered what Tom would taste like?

Hunter snapped his fingers in front of my face and said, "Wake up, Sister! Did you? Did he? Whaaat happened?"

"He kissed me! No, that's not right. He went to kiss me, and I stopped him!" I took hold of Hunter's hands and jumped up and down on the spot while he joined in.

"Why are we so excited if you didn't kiss?" he asked, frowning.

"Come through to my bedroom and I'll sort out your face and tell you all about it. Wee, I'm so excited my heart is pumping like a steam train! But you're giving me the creeps with makeup spread all over your mush and a scowl on your face."

"I don't scowl. Ever!" He pouted.

I plonked him down on my chair and grabbed a cotton wool ball from the side. "I'm starting again. You look like a circus clown. What have you been doing?"

"Well, it didn't look this bad until you came in hugging me and making me get up close and personal with the window."

"You did that on your own. I never made you hang out of the window and blow kisses to my boyfriend. Oh, God, oh God. Does this mean you were right? I'm going to get my man?"

"Hang on, Honey, one flyby doesn't make you the destination." He shook his finger at my reflection in the mirror.

The smile dropped from my face. "Am I reading too much into this?"

"I don't know. Tell me everything!"

After I'd finished telling him about my day, the only comment he made was, "Promising. I think you should go to the club with me tonight."

"Oh, I think I'll give it a miss. I'm shattered. In fact, my legs are already aching. Is Susie back home yet? I thought I'd spend a bit of time with her."

Hunter screwed up his mouth. "No, she's still sulking."

"Give her a few more days and she'll get fed up staying at her boyfriend's. It wouldn't hurt if you apologised about the fat thing," I said.

"I might eventually, but not yet. I'm still nursing a thorn in my heart at what she said about me being a fake. Anyway, it's alright for her running to her boyfriend and making love every night, where I have to live my sad, lonely life."

"At least someone's making love to you."

"God Beth, it wasn't lovemaking. Smacking my arse until it glowed and then getting me to crawl on my hands and knees to beg for it is only sex. Great sex, but definitely not lovemaking. I wish it were."

I clapped a hand to my head. "TMI Hunter!"

"You'll come to the club tonight, please?" he begged.

I turned his face to mine. "Is something the matter?"

"Lola's playing hard to get. You may get your man, but I don't think I'll get mine. I think he only wants me for sex."

"And you're still sleeping with him?" I asked, gob smacked.

"No, but he's shagging my brains out."

I wrapped my arms around him and held him tight. My brow crumpled. He didn't even complain about me ruining his makeup.

"I can't say no, Beth. I feel like such a tramp."

I paused, conflicted by what to say. Any other time, and I would have described Hunter as just that, but I hadn't known him to sleep with another person in the last seven months. This wasn't the norm for Hunter, he didn't do relationships. He never slept with anyone longer than a few months and then he was on to the next conquest. Either Liam was the smartest cookie in the jar and was playing the long game to capture and solidify Hunter's feelings or he was toying with him. And I couldn't tell which.

"I'll come to the club tonight. Will you stick a pizza in the oven while I have a soak?"

"Oh, you're coming?" He wiggled his eyebrows, and I groaned. "Let me go and a make dis a pizza for the beautiful lady."

"Grazie," I said, kissing him on both cheeks.

"And Beth, if Lola or Liam come near me, can you jump in there and stop him from taking me to the broom cupboard or up the back alley? I need you to be my chastity belt tonight, sweetness. I can't keep crumbling to this man's demands."

"Are you sure that's what you want?"

"I want him to take me seriously."

"Okay, I'll do what I can."

***

I'd been trailing around after Hunter all night, as

though I was his shadow, so I was glad to take a breather and sit at the bar while he performed. Lola, in the early part of the evening, had her own personal set and had spent most of the night dashing between the stage and the dressing room for a quick change. Propped on a chair near Hunter's dressing table, I had a bird's-eye view of the entire area and in between touching up one of the girl's makeup, to hopping back on my pedestal, I watched Lola's moves surreptitiously from my perch. So far, I hadn't had to do too much fending off to save Hunter's virtue.

It was as though Lola understood precisely why I was here tonight. Apart from a quick greeting hug when he entered the dressing room, it was almost as if Hunter had become invisible to him.

As I sat on a barstool with a glass of fizz in my hand, it surprised me to find Liam at my elbow. I looked down and my mouth fell open. Hunter was right. Liam out of drag was a completely different kettle of fish – a delightful dish.

In slow motion, I watched as Liam dragged a stool nearer to me and asked, "Evening Beth, do you mind if I take a seat next to you?"

"No, not at all," I stuttered.

The bartender came over and slid a glass of clear liquid to Liam with a nod and left to serve a punter without charging him.

"Do you have a tab?" I asked.

Liam lifted the glass and said, "It's only tap water. I'm too much of a control freak to drink alcohol. Cheers. To friends and a great fuck."

I pursed my lips and was about to hop off my chair when Liam's hand caught my elbow.

"Sorry, I shouldn't have said that. I was being flippant, because you make me nervous."

I swung around and looked at his expression. What I saw had me settle back down in my seat. "Why would I make you nervous? I wouldn't say that you were a nervous person."

"I'm not, but you're Hunter's best friend." He looked over to the stage where he was performing with the other girls. "If you don't like me, that will be game over for him and me."

"You hang too much weight on my approval. Hunter's a big boy. He can make his own mind up."

"If that's true, why are you here tonight? We both know it's not to do the girl's makeup. Not that anyone's going to complain if you do. Skills like yours don't grow on trees."

I shook my head. "Never mind what I'm doing. What are you playing at with my friend?"

"Would you like another drink?"

"No, I want to know how you feel about Hunter, because right now he's suffering, and I hate to see it."

Liam ran a hand through his hair. "God, that wasn't my intention."

"Then what is your intention?" I drew my eyebrows together and threw up my hands.

"I'm giving him what he wants, no strings attached, great sex. You know Hunter, he's a fly by night, a love-them-and-leave-them kind of guy. I don't want to be another notch on his bedpost. I want more. Do you think if I'd started a proper relationship with him, he'd still be here? When the novelty of banging a dwarf faded, would there'd be anything left?"

"But you've been friends for years. Your relationship isn't just based on sex, you have a solid base," I said, crossing my hands over my chest and staring him down.

"I'm not the first friend to cross the line, Beth. Oh, don't get me wrong, he's kept those friendships on the whole, but after a quick fling, they're all relegated to the friend's zone."

"So that's your plan; to keep him dangling on a string, while you lead him around by the balls until what?"

Liam's face dropped. Grasping his hands together he said, "Until he loves me."

I took hold of Liam's hand and said gently, "And how will you know that?"

Everyone noticed Hunter missed another cue and the nudge, and whispers of admonishment from the Queens, but nobody knew the reason, apart from me. I looked at the stage and smiled at him; he threw up his arms in triumph, beaming, with tears glistening in his eyes.

CHAPTER 27

TOM

Driving home, all I could think of was Jane's comment on parting. I threw the parking ticket on the passenger seat and sang along to the radio, running over the words in my head until I clipped a traffic cone and got it wedged under my front bumper. Eventually, I had to stop the car and remove it. I looked at a smooth portion of the white circling the orange and thought it reminded me of the tone of Jane's skin. Grinning to myself, I hugged it to me and considered taking it back to my apartment before common sense kicked in, and I laid it down carefully by the side of the road.

The rest of the journey, I attempted to concentrate on what was around me and banish all thoughts of Jane from my head before I had an accident involving something more substantial than a traffic cone, but everything reminded me of her in some small way. A cyclist riding along had me grinning from ear to ear. A woman chasing after a child made me think back to her with Cassie and Jahan, and a workman with purple pants showing the crack of his arse made me focus on how much cleavage she had on display today.

By the time I arrived home, I was ready to wash my

mouth out with bleach and return to her flat. But Harry would have brought Drago back from his walk, and he'd need a bit of company before I even considered going out again. His face had pulled at my heartstrings when I'd left him this morning, but as I'd passed Harry on my way out, it reassured me that Drago's frown would soon be turned upside down when Harry entered. Much thumping and excited yelping had followed his high-five on opening my apartment door.

As I turned the key in the lock, my phone pinged twice. Pushing open the door, I looked at the screen and read the first message.

"Drago wanted to stay around mine for a sleepover. Enjoy the rest of your day and night. H."

I smirked. So, it was Drago's idea, was it?

I flicked down to the second message and leaned my back on the door. Taking a breath, I reread it and looked around the empty apartment. It was time to put my plan into action. First things first, go clean your teeth and sit and chill for a bit. I picked up my phone and typed in 'how safe would it be to kiss someone with a food allergy?' Four hours, great! 'And clean your teeth', tick.

I flipped on my console and booted up Universal War Warriors - anything to take my mind off going to the Trap Door later. As the game loaded, I hopped up and dashed into the kitchen, grabbed a dish out of my freezer and bunged it in the microwave. I could have cooked myself something, but it was easier to grab a dinner that my nutritionist had made for me, perfectly balanced in protein, veg and low in fat. If I cooked for myself, I'd probably have made good old bacon and eggs and then gone in search of something sweet to fill me up.

After waging war for a few hours, I headed for my bathroom, showered, and took extra care to soap around my mouth, rubbing the bubbles into my lips until I'd swallowed some, I spat out the acrid apple flavour and rinsed my tongue with water.

As I wrapped a towel around my waist and glanced in the mirror, I studied my teeth and tongue for any traces of food. Taking out my toothbrush, I cleaned them, and then brought out a fancy water system flossing gadget from my cupboard I'd used twice before and went over them again. Flipping my shaving mirror to high magnification, I examined my mouth until I was sure it was spotlessly clean, and gave my reflection a satisfied smile, flicked the towel from my waist and wiggled my hips. "Looking good, Austin." I said, winking at the cocky bastard staring back at me. With that, I dressed and headed out the door.

***

On entering the Trap Door, I looked around me, trying to get my bearings. After a moment, I spotted Hunter in full drag, centre stage. He was in the middle of a sexy number, emulating some fashion pop icon, and doing a surprisingly good job of it, even though the star was at least a foot shorter than him and female. He clocked me looking and nudged his head towards the bar, where Jane sat with the handsomest midget I'd seen in my life.

I glanced back over at Hunter as I threaded my way

through the packed club and nodded as he waggled his finger at me in a clear, keep off he's mine, look. I smirked and mimed; no worries, he's all yours. Halfway to the bar, a hand grabbed my arse and gave it a squeeze. A guy with a beautifully painted face leaned forward and purred in my ear, "Hey gorgeous, want to disrobe a lady and find out her deepest secret?"

I looked down at the guy's bulge under his satin dress. "Yep, that one over there," I said pointing towards Jane. "I think Bletchley Park wouldn't be hard pushed to uncover yours."

She fluttered her eyelashes and followed my finger to where Jane sat. "Beth? You're with Beth?" she asked in a gruff, masculine voice.

"A guy can but hope," I said, walking on.

A wave of interest radiated from the guy as though a pebble had dropped into a pool of water. By the time I'd reached Jane and the dwarf, it appeared the entire room knew my intentions and was trying to hide their obvious interest.

Jane glanced up and froze as the dwarf slipped off his stool and offered it to me.

"Wow, you make quite an entrance, don't you, Mr Rochester?" Jane grinned.

I turned around and viewed the sea of faces looking at us instead of the stage.

"They weren't interested in me until I mentioned I'd come here to see you," I said.

The dwarf gestured to the bar staff, and they handed over a microphone at his request.

"Hey, you bunch of Queens and Princesses, did you come here to watch the show and flaunt those fabulous bodies? Or snoop on other people's business?"

A rumble spread through the crowd, and a few patrons edged back towards the stage.

"Beth's been good to us. It's time to give her some space. Josphine, pump out those dance tunes. Hunter and I are going to do a duet!"

There was an enormous cheer from the crowd as midget fought his way back to the stage. After a second, the audience formed a pathway and Hunter whipped off his long dress to reveal a sexy gold leotard. He grabbed Liam the moment he reached him and threw him about as though he were a circus acrobat.

For a moment, Jane and I stared, mouths hanging open, and then the crowd started jumping up and down, to the music.

I slid into the seat beside her and said, "What just happened here?"

Jane grinned. "I guess the entire club was waiting for those two to get together."

"Hunter and the handsome dwarf?" I asked.

"Hunter and Liam." Jane corrected me gently. "I think that dance represents their relationship reaching the next level."

"They're going to become lovers?"

"Oh no. They've been lovers for months. Now, they're going to date."

I shook my head. "Okay, I think I get it. Would you

like a drink?" I swung the seat around to face the bar and brushed my knee against hers. My heart thudded in my chest just at the brief contact.

"Please, I'm on the bubbly."

"Champagne or lemonade?" I asked.

"Neither Prosecco. I'm treating the aches with alcohol."

I turned to the barman and ordered our drinks.

"So, how did you know I'd be here tonight?" Jane asked.

"A little bird told me."

"Hunter, little bird my foot."

I watched her throw a disapproving look towards the stage as I handed over her drink.

"You didn't mind, did you?" I asked, shifting in my seat. "I felt I owed you a kiss. One that wouldn't kill you or give you a trout pout." I grimaced, thinking I'd gone too far as I watched the different emotions race across her face. "It would be safe now. I looked it up and washed my mouth out with bleach." I took in her horrified expression and said, "I am joking, although the apple shower gel tasted awful, and I cleaned my teeth twice." I glanced at my watch. "And it said it would be safe after four hours and it's already been six."

"Apple did you say, Mr Rochester?" she said, backing away from me as if I had the plague.

"God, you're not allergic to apples too, are you? Please tell me you're not. It tasted nothing like an apple. I'm not sure it was even related to one. And I sprayed the shower in my mouth for a good five minutes to get rid of the taste, so..."

She reached forward and cupped my jaw. "Dear Mr Rochester, I was only teasing you."

I leaned forward and placed my lips on hers, moulded into the soft sweetness of her mouth, and felt my body spring to life as she placed her other hand on my thigh. Then I pulled back to catch my breath.

A crinkle formed between her brows. "I'm sorry, I'm out of practice," she said.

"Out of practice? God help me if you were on top form. I've always said you've got a wonderful touch. Who knew that included your lips?"

She chuckled and flushed the colour of a pink lady apple.

"Ah, Jane, you have no idea what you do to me. I can hardly imagine what it would be like with you in my bed."

"Bed?" She took a hearty slurp of her drink. "I'm not getting naked with you Tom. I'd have to be really drunk for that!"

"What? Why? I like you; you like me. Or don't you like me in that way?" I asked, the bottom dropping out of my world. "I'm not rushing you, Jane. If you need more time?" I hoped my face didn't let me down on that one.

"No, it's not so much that. I mean, of course I like you in that way. God, I've still got a pulse. It's just..." She dropped her head. "You're Beauty, I'm the Beast, but even this beast has a heart, and you could so easily break it."

"Jane, stop, please. I don't see you like that. You're the

kindest, funniest, quirkiest, sweet person I know. Kiss me again and I'll show you."

"Oh Rochester, no amount of kissing is going to turn this frog into a prince."

"I hope not. I'm not into guys." I ordered another drink and took hold of her hand, threading my fingers through hers. "I'm serious Jane, I want us to date. Not just a fling, a proper relationship."

I watched as she chewed on her lip. "Okay, we'll try it. But if you and I ever get naked, I'm going to be drunk as a skunk or you're going to be blindfolded."

Considering her words, I shrugged. "I'd rather you weren't paralytic. I'd like you to remember our first time, and not be able to say afterwards that you only slept with me because I got you drunk."

CHAPTER 28

BETH

When Tom said those words, at first, I was ready to walk away, as if I would ever say that about such a special moment in our lives? Admittedly, it was my lack of self-belief that made me need protection from his gaze, afraid I'd see the image of myself reflected in his eyes, And I knew to be true that I was as far from perfect as Elizabeth Bennet can get when compared to Tom Austin.

Who would believe that he would ever have to get a woman drunk just so she would sleep with him? And then I realised that in the celebrity fame game, it didn't matter, because the press weren't after the truth, they were after a story. And that would make a sensational one. One that could, if spun right, ruin his career, even though in his heart he must know that I would never do that. How many times had he put his trust in others, only for them to let him down? Fame was a world of mist and illusion, where an ordinary person became something close to a God. Tom played superheroes and men with extraordinary powers and there was a part of the world that believed he was capable of the things his characters could do. Even behind the attractive veneer, beat a heart that pumped blood around his body, the same as everyone else, and would ache with the loss of a loved one just as fiercely. He had insecurities the same as you or me. When I thought back, I remembered how he had wanted me to tell him how good an actor he was, and when I rejected him in the car, he thought it was because my affections no longer laid with him but with his best friend Rivers.

"Okay, I'm not making any promises. Remember, I've all but seen you naked, and it's pretty intimidating for a girl like me. Walk me home, Tom. I'm shattered." I said, about to slip off the stool and saunter out. But that wasn't how it happened. My leg muscles cramped from the shock of horse riding for the first time in ten years and acted like the world's largest cargo ship being guided out of the smallest port by a five-year-old child. After a couple of attempts, I removed my bottom from the chair and half slid, half bumped my way to the floor. There I, bow-legged, waddled across the room, exiting the doors and made my way across the lobby.

"Need any help there?" Tom asked, trying to stifle a laugh.

"No. Whoever had the idea of horse riding after a decade needs to be shot."

He held his hands up and grinned. "I don't suppose that fall helped much, either?"

"Don't remind me. My bum feels as though it's made of lead. Painful lead."

His face sobered. "I'm so sorry about that, Jane. I feel responsible. If I hadn't been stupid enough to date Alisha. This would never have happened to you. I…"

I pushed my finger to his mouth. God, even my arms ached. "Ssh, Tom, none of it was your fault. How could you have possibly known what a crazy woman she was?"

I watched as his eyes softened and his shoulders drooped, filled with remorse.

"Tom," I said, cupping his face with my hands and guiding it to mine. I kissed that strong, full mouth, savouring his taste, relishing the touch of his lips, gently caressing mine. And then he deepened the kiss, his tongue invading my mouth. Sending my senses reeling as I pressed my body into his and felt his arousal nudge my stomach. My hands dropped and wound their way around his waist, melting into him. My breath hitched as I felt his heartbeat hammer in his chest. His fingers delved into my hair, cradling the back of my nape as he expertly deepened the kiss further until I was drowning in the essence of this beautiful man. We stumbled back against the door as I wrapped one leg around his ankle.

"Wow, what a show tonight! First Hunter throwing Liam around like a firecracker and now you two giving us an X-rated show in the foyer. Hold that thought while I get a comfortable chair," said the doorman.

Tom and I sprung apart, laughing like children.

"God, that was hot, Jane," Tom said, adjusting his trousers. "How do you feel about coming back to my place for a nightcap?"

I wrapped my hand around his fingers and led him out of the club. Away from the security cameras.

"I'm not that sort of girl, Tom."

He pulled out of my grasp and turned his back on me, walking a few steps away and then doubled back, running his hand through his hair. "Ass," he bit out.

I dropped my gaze and wrung my hands together. "I'm sorry, Tom, It's not…"

At the same time, he said, "Me, not you. I meant I was an ass." He stepped forward and grasped my hands. "I'm sorry Jane, I've told you I wanted a proper relationship and then act like a dick."

My mouth curved. "That's alright Mr Rochester, you're used to being a dick."

He pulled me closer. "Yes, you're right, I am. It's been years since I've had to work hard to get a girl."

"They usually fall at your feet."

"Yes. But I don't want that with you." He put his hands up. "I lie. Of course, I want *that*! I want all of you, when you're ready to give it. Until then, can we just get to know each other better? Come back to mine. I promise I won't touch you! Maybe a kiss. Although mainly to talk and spend some time together. What do you say? Give me a chance to show you I'm one of the good guys?"

I stood rooted to the spot; I knew what type of guy he was. Whether he was the right guy remained to be seen. My heart told me yes, but my head. Well, my head had a hundred-page dossier with all the cons.

I shook my head, but my hand found his and we walked down the pavement, until he hailed a passing black cab and climbed in. He gave his address, then sat back in his seat, gazed out the window, and I watched the muscles in his jaw working. His thumb raked across the top of my hand as though he were trying to rub an uncomfortable thought away.

"What's up Rochester?" I asked, stilling his thumb

with my other hand.

His face turned to mine; surprise written across his features. "Nothing, I was miles away." He smiled, but it didn't reach his eyes.

"There's got to be something. I can almost hear your jaw muscles ping under the strain."

He shifted in his seat. "You're far too perceptive, Jane." Looking at the back of the cabbie's head, he slid the glass partition across so the driver couldn't hear us. "I was thinking about that fiasco today. What was the point of it? Was Alisha just trying to hurt you, or did she have an ulterior motive? I mean, if she was trying to hurt you, that was bad enough, but it's never that simple with that witch."

I gave his hand a squeeze. "It's okay Tom, I'm fine, and whatever tomorrow brings, if anything, we'll weather it together. Tonight, let's enjoy what we have."

He brought my hand to his lips and kissed it. "How do you put up with me?"

"Oh, I struggle. Although, I remember you didn't get away scot-free this morning. How are your unmentionables?"

His smile crumpled. "My unmentionables are tender. Back to where they should be after being catapulted to the heavens, but in need of kissing. Hell, did I just say that out loud?"

I chortled. "I'm not sure I should return home with you. You obviously haven't got your mind or other things on friendship." I looked down at his groin accusingly.

"I have, but other parts of me haven't. Can't you tell

I'm powerless and completely at the mercy of my sword? It has a will of its own."

"And there was me thinking superheroes could control their special powers."

"They probably can, but I'm only a man."

"Shame, I could do with a hero who knows how to wield his sword."

"Stop Jane. All this teasing is causing me to chafe."

I grinned. "You can sit naked while we talk if you like? I won't hold it against you if you're in discomfort. If you're uncomfortable being naked, I'm sure we can find a sock!"

"Jane," he growled. "Stop tormenting the inflicted."

I stroked his thigh, and he groaned, "The bloody horse whisperers back." He gritted his teeth. "Are you doing this on purpose?"

"Who me? Don't you like your leg being rubbed?"

"Grr, of course I do, but then so do the bits I'm trying hard to remind that tonight is only platonic."

"Oh dear! I should stop then?" I said, taking my hand away.

"Yes. No, I'll suffer the consequences," he said, putting my hand firmly back on his thigh.

"So brave." I sighed dreamily at him. "My hero."

"I hope that means I've earned a reward?"

CHAPTER 29

TOM

I opened the door to my apartment, letting Jane wander in front of me as my lights automatically switched on, brightening the way.

"Where's Drago?" she asked, looking over her shoulder at me.

"He's around my brother Harry's, having a sleepover."

"Oh, a shame. Still, at least he's not home alone. You haven't been here much today." She nudged her shoes off and left them neatly by the door. "Your apartment's beautiful. Older than I thought and kind of homely. How come you use an ordinary key when you have these lighting gadgets? I thought you'd have a retinal scanner or something?"

"Thanks. It should be. It cost me an absolute fortune. Property's so expensive here, and there's only Drago and me most of the time. As for the key, that's my choice. I'm a bit of a traditionalist in some ways, and there's enough security in the lobby." I held up the key. "Can't beat something that's worked perfectly for centuries."

She nodded and walked in, her hand moving from

surface-to-surface, trailing over an award, a bronze of a dog running through grass. Then onto a marble vase and a bookcase, fingering each spine as though a caress. I cleared my throat and adjusted myself. How I wished I were those items beneath that sensual touch of hers. Ridiculous to be jealous of an inanimate object, but my body ached as each pad of her finger smoothed along every pathway.

"Do you mind?" she asked, as she made her way around my apartment. Examining all my fittings as though she was in church.

"No, make yourself at home. That leads out onto the patio."

"You have a patio here?"

"It's Drago's mainly. Kind of necessity when you have a dog. In my LA home, he has a big garden."

"Two homes? Sometimes I forget how famous you are."

"Forget entirely Jane, if it helps."

"Helps what?" She turned and looked at me.

"Helps you see me as an ordinary person. Would you like a drink?" I asked, heading into the kitchen.

She left the window where she stood holding my curtain and followed me through. "Tea, please, if you have it?" She sat on a stool and worried her lip. "I *do* see you as an ordinary person, but someone who is in extraordinary circumstances."

"Is that what you'd call my job?" I asked, as I took down two cups and flicked the kettle on.

"No, not your job. I'm talking about fame, the press, the social whirl around everything you do. The hunger to know everything about you and those that surround you. Sometimes it must be stifling."

"It is what it is. You can't listen to all the voices, otherwise you'd go mad. Fame has a price to pay and obviously I had the choice to pursue this life. You, if you're with me, won't be in such a fortunate position."

"The Beast of Bermondsey?" She stood up and took the cup I offered.

I left my mug on the side and walked behind her, wrapping my arms around her waist. "Oh, I hope so. It would be boring if you were just a plain old pussycat."

She chuckled. "Would it now, Mr Rochester?"

"Yes. Oh no, it's no good. Got to put some joggers on. All this talk of beastly pursuits has me hard pressed."

I nipped off to change. The talk of animal was making me ache, and I wasn't sure how much of that was hitting the saddle hard this morning, or how much was Jane having other effects on me. Well, this is a turnaround from me thinking I didn't fancy her. Now, I can't think about anything apart from her running her hands over me, and when she calls me Rochester and that mischievous dimple appears – Lord have mercy, for I have sinned!

When I came back from my bedroom, hanging loose in baggy jogging pants and nothing else, I found Jane on my sofa, game controller in her hand, our cups on the coffee table in front of the telly. I dropped my hands, hiding my arousal. Who would have thought seeing a woman with a controller in her hand and cups placed thoughtfully on the table would cause such a reaction? Certainly not me. It had never happened before in the thirty-odd years of playing video games.

Her cheeks glowed a rosy hue. I grinned, thinking it was because I had my chiselled chest out, but her next statement made me wonder if I lived in cloud cuckoo land.

"I hope you don't mind. You told me to make myself at home," she said, waving the controller about and staring at my bare feet.

Higher! My mind screamed. My feet are ordinary. I looked down at them and frowned. They were decent ones as feet go, not too hairy and nicely proportioned. When my gaze lifted, I found Jane wearing a similar frown to mine. Was she thinking my feet were pretty awesome too?

"You don't mind, do you?" Jane put the controller on the coffee table, grasping her fingers together.

"Oh!" I laughed. "No, of course I don't mind. So, do you like to play video games?" I sat down beside her and picked up a controller.

"Sometimes, yes. What are you playing?"

"I'm kind of a geek when it comes to computer games. Something like a D and D enthusiast, but I can't stop playing Universal War Warriors. I even make and paint all the characters, look over there in the cabinet."

Jane chuckled. "Who ever thought you'd be a game geek?" She got up and peered in. "They're really good. I noticed them when I came in, but I never realised you made them. Isn't that Urdak and Beft I see in there?"

I sat forward in my seat and fiddled with the controller buttons restlessly. "Yes."

She glanced over her shoulder and laughed. "You're itching to play, aren't you? Think you're going to beat me, huh?"

I gnawed on my lip. Blasted woman had to keep coming out with these suggestive remarks. Of course I wanted to play! Video games, I reminded myself. I forced myself to get up and walk stiffly over to the cabinet. "Yes, I think I can beat you, Jane. You've obviously played UWW before, but I'm a master."

"Ho ho! Cocky aren't we? I can conquer all, worm," she said in a voice unnervingly close to mine in Ironclaw.

"Did that just come from you?" I asked, catching flies. She nodded, a curve to her lips. "Oh, you are so going down!" God, now it's me with the double entendre. "I'm mean I'm going to..." Beat. nail, show you... "Win."

She put her head on one side, a quizzical look on her face and shook her head and said, "Game on!"

We dashed around to the other side of the coffee table and grabbed the controllers.

"Which character do you want to be?" I asked, flicking through the menu.

"I don't mind. Whoever you don't want to be."

I put the controller down and rubbed my hands together. "Fighting talk! I'm usually Beft. Let's see, who shall I choose for you? You're small and shy, kind of surprising... I know, Mouse."

"You're underestimating me already Mr Rochester. Presuming I'm timid, just because I'm shy, and Mouse is a young boy. People always think he's a pushover."

"Ah, but he can get the same weapons as all the other characters."

"Yes, I know. I know just where to find them, too." Her mouth curved up and there was a glint in her eye.

"You've been Mouse before, haven't you?" I asked, looking at her out of the corner of my eye.

"Once or twice. I usually let men I play with choose, and they always give me Mouse. You fellas are creatures of habit."

"How many men have you played with Jane?" I said in a low warning voice.

She lifted an eyebrow. "Now, let's see, I'm thirty-one now. I started when I was...? Erm?"

I watched her face closely.

"Let's see, was it while I was at college or after I left? No, I was still at school."

I swallowed. "How young Jane?" Lord, please don't tell me she was the school bike.

"Twelve."

"Twelve? As in one and two? A dozen, by the stroke of?" I think I was panting by this time; the coffee table came rushing up to meet me and I put my hand out to steady myself. "You jest with me, Jane?"

"No, I started playing UWW when I was twelve. Mum and Dad were always at work and my elder brother let me do whatever I wanted."

"But it's an eighteen plus game!"

"Yes, I know, but Matt is six years older than me, and at first, when he found out I was using his console he was really mad. Thought I'd mucked everything up." She rolled her eyes. "Silly boy. Anyway, are we going to start this game or not?"

"Yes, we'll talk more of this later."

CHAPTER 30

BETH

Dazed from how often Tom touched me, I sighed with relief when he went to change into something more comfortable. Isn't that the woman's line? I rolled my eyes at myself and went to explore his lounge. I'd already spotted the gaming figures mid-fight in the display cabinet and my hands were itching to take up a controller and fight with a worthy opponent. As I expected Tom to be with the level of commitment, he'd shown in collecting such fine figures. They were really exquisite. Still, I expected he could afford decent ones at a price.

Then, when he walked in wearing only jogging pants and nothing else, and I mean nothing else. I nearly choked on my saliva. The man might as well have been naked. For a second, fireworks went off in my head and a few other places. Then I had the good sense to look at his feet. A safer option than the rest of him, which made lava seem decidedly icy in comparison.

Play it cool Beth, I urged myself. He's used to people ogling. I concentrated on the game, desperate to take my mind away from this god, now sat beside me, but everything he said appeared to have a different meaning. I smiled at him, gripping the controller. "Are we playing or not?" I heard myself ask.

Five minutes later, I'd found a stash of weapons and was heading back to the battlefield. Carnage surrounded us as our opposing sides battled it out. I took a quick breath as I saw Tom's character, Beft, push his way through the crowd and take up a fighting stance in front of me. I grinned to myself, rookie mistake underestimating someone smaller and quicker. Mouse dropped to the ground, swinging his legs out and felled Beft in one move. In an instant, I was on his chest, a short dagger at his throat. This was way too easy!

Tom's character pulled the dagger toward him, then agilely flipped us over, using his full weight to pin Mouse down. I had been expecting this, so I rolled on my side and before we knew it, we were rolling around like a wheel. My dagger fell from my grasp, and I scrambled Mouse to his feet. Pulling a long sword from my back, before Beft had the chance to find his feet. Although Tom craftily played my move back to me, swinging his character's feet to take out my ankles and have me unarmed, on my back in seconds.

It wasn't long before both characters were weaponless and at a stalemate. Tom glanced at me, sweat trickling down his temple and coating his skin with a sugared coating any girl with a sweet tooth would have found hard to resist.

"Want to go hand to hand combat? Think that's unfair though, Beft's much bigger and stronger than Mouse," he said, wiping a hand over his face and through his hair.

"Sure," I said, wiping my hands down my trousers,

eager for the next round.

"Lord, don't say you're an expert at that too?"

"Oh, Mr Rochester, a girl has to learn how to defend herself." I winked. "It's a dangerous world out there."

"Huh, I'm not sure who for! How come you haven't even broken into a sweat?"

"It's not me doing the exercise, Tom, it's the character. You're only nervous because a girl might beat you." I smirked.

"How can someone as uncoordinated as you be so good at this?"

"What gave you the idea I'm uncoordinated?"

"You got on a horse backward," he said, drily.

"I was nervous. I hadn't ridden for ten years!"

"You came in the first day wearing a polka dot bra, with oil in your hair."

"It was dark, and that was a hair treatment, which I had an allergic reaction to. Anyway, none of those things hinted I was dextrously challenged, just unlucky."

"Okay, accident prone is more accurate." He nodded.

I tilted my head to the side and thought back to everything that had happened since I'd known him - I guess he had a point. "Alright, I'll concede that point, but not this contest. You're going down Beft, down in the dirt, until you kiss my feet."

"I'd rather kiss your mouth," Tom muttered, picking his controller back up. "I like you, but I'm not letting you win this one Jane. The kid gloves are off. Now you'll be the one kissing my feet."

"Oh, I don't think so. I have no intention of getting close to those horrible, ugly things. Shall we?" I turned to the screen, trying to hide a smile.

"Hey, what's wrong with my feet?" he asked, waving one about in my line of sight.

"Ugh, put it down or better still, put some socks on."

"I have nice feet," Tom said stubbornly.

"Beauty's in the eye of the beholder!" I guided Mouse around the back of Beft, kneeing him in the back of the leg and watched him crumple to the ground.

Tom's head popped up from his feet. "Hey cheat! Taking advantage of a man when he's at his most vulnerable."

"Oh, how I'd like to take advantage of you," I whispered, unable to keep the smile from my face.

"Jane, stop teasing me. It's putting me off my game."

"My tactics are working, then?" Beft was just on his feet when Mouse roundhouse kicked him in the chest and watched the giant fall as though he was a Redwood. "Timber," I cried.

"I never thought you would be so ruthless and underhanded," he said, fake pouting.

"I seem to remember hearing this warrior say, 'Don't be too proud to take every advantage, especially when you're fighting at a disadvantage. Pride will get you killed'."

"Wherever did you hear that stupid bit of advice

from?" he asked.

Mouse gave Beft a punch to his throat and flipped him onto his front, pinning his hands behind his back as he sat on him.

I chuckled, sneaking a peep at Tom. "You as Ironclaw," I said.

"Oh shit, you're beating me at my own game," he groaned dramatically as Beft bucked, throwing Mouse high enough to release his hands.

But expecting the move, I said, "Check." Mouse rolled and grabbed a stray shield from the battleground and bashed it down on Beft's head. The giant's face landed in the dirt, splashing up droplets of muddy water as his face went slack. "Mate," I said with a flourish from my controller.

Tom sat there with his mouth open. "Brutal," he said at last.

"How does it feel, going down at the hands of a girl?" I crowed.

He smirked. "Did you say, going down on a..."

I clapped a hand over his mouth and shook my head. "friends", I mouthed as he winced.

"Ah, doesn't the loser get a booby prize?" he asked innocently.

I shook my head firmly. "Most definitely not."

"Fancy some popcorn?" he asked, breaking the tension.

***

We played UWW three more times until he beat me, and then he didn't stop telling me what a loser I was. I flicked a piece of popcorn at his head and told him he was a jerk, which only made him retaliate by bombarding me with corn kernels. Eventually one stuck to his chest, so I leant forward and plucked it off him with my mouth, but he rolled onto his back, taking me with him, so I ended up lying on him. I looked up into his face and pushed myself off his chest.

"Ahem, sorry. I guess that was too close up and personal?" I said. Remaining in his arms.

"Jane," he said, brushing a piece of hair away from my face with his finger. "I said I wouldn't *touch* you, not that I wouldn't kiss you."

I looked into his eyes, drowning in the islands of gold and green and felt for a minute like an astronaut gazing down onto the Earth from the bleakness of space. I stroked my hand up his jaw, running my thumb over his bottom lip as both of us held our breaths while our heartbeats hammered in our chests.

"Tom, I..."

His mouth closed on mine, tentative, exploring. My fingers reached up into his hair as I inched up his body. For a long time, our kisses remained soft, sweet and then hunger took over and he delved in deeper, probing with his tongue as I greedily joined him, desperate to get as close to him as I could. He lavished my mouth with gentle pecks, then power and passion took over once more, bruising my lips and creating a fire in my belly. Time drifted on until the soft hues of morning crept through the clouds and snuck shadows of dancing light around the room. Eventually, the kisses became whispers of caresses across our skin, dancing at our faces, throats and chests. I lowered my head onto his torso and listened to the comforting thud of his heart. Sometime in the night, or early morning, I must have fallen asleep on Tom's sofa. On Tom himself, my arms wrapped around his body.

Some hours later, I awoke. A pool of saliva stuck the side of my face to his chest and as I gently parted us, I stared into his face, caught my breath as I watched the way his eyelashes kissed his cheeks and his features relaxed in repose were as tempting as when he was awake.

"Nur nama," he murmured in his sleep.

I smiled down at him and with reluctance slid from his body. He huffed softly and turned on his side, missing my warmth. I tiptoed towards the door, pausing by his bedroom. Pushed it open and snuck in, grabbed a blanket from the end of his bed, I returned to drape it over him, then slipped on my shoes and left.

CHAPTER 31

TOM

The scratch of a key turning in my door stirred me from my slumber. I listened to the sound of Drago's feet scrabbling across the wooden floor and Harry encouraging him to be quiet as he crept past my bedroom door, giggling like a schoolgirl. I sat up on my sofa and rubbed the sleep from my eyes. When had I fallen asleep, and why wasn't I in my bed? Then the night before came flooding back.

Harry stood bolt upright when he saw me on the sofa. "Where's your date?" he asked as Drago jumped onto my lap.

I lifted his paw off my groin and screwed up my face. Everything appeared normal, yet the person I most wanted to see had disappeared into thin air.

"Huh?" I asked Harry, rubbing a hand over my stubble and then looked down at my chest where something clear and sticky sat, matting my chest hair together. I smiled down at the evidence that I hadn't dreamed all of last night. Jane had been here, cuddled up against my body. I peeked under the blanket and nodded, still wearing bottoms; I hadn't seduced her. That bit was merely a dream. I looked around me. Where had she gone? Was she in the bathroom? I moved Drago to one side and tossed the blanket off. "Was there a pair of shoes by the door?" I asked.

"Only yours mate. No killer heels." Harry smirked.

"Shit, has she gone?" I asked, looking around me.

Harry full out laughed. "Don't tell me a girl has walked out on you? That's got to be a first!"

"Why would she do that? It doesn't make any sense," I said to myself, frowning as I ran a hand through my hair.

"Perhaps now you're getting older, you're losing your charm, old boy?" he said.

"Get lost Harry. This isn't any girl we're talking about; this is Jane!"

"The beast?" His eyebrows rose, and I could all but see the cogs turning in his brain.

I'd told Harry a bit about her. How Alisha had taken advantage of me knocking her off her bike and sold the story to the papers. I'd mentioned that we were friends, but not much else. There wasn't much more to tell.

I groaned. "Don't call her that. Jane's too good a person to be stuck with that moniker."

Harry took hold of my arm. "Hang on one minute. Are you telling me that Jane stayed here last night? Did you, you know?" he asked, raising his eyebrows at me.

"No. Fuck, why am I even answering you? It's none of your business." I walked over and shut the front door. "Don't you ever close a fucking door?" I said, walking back into the living room.

"Whoa, who got up on the wrong side of the couch this morning? Just because you never got your leg over."

"It's not that you moron. I'm not sure I would have been fit for that anyway," I muttered.

Smiling, he asked, "Why not? Did someone hit you in the knackers with a cricket bat?"

I winced. "Close enough."

"Oh man, that sucks. Is that why she left early?" he asked, sitting on my sofa as he draped an arm around Drago's shoulder and shook out a newspaper in his other hand.

"You picked up a paper on your way round?" I asked with a sneer on my lips.

"Some of us like to catch up on the world around us," Harry said, crossing his legs and making himself comfortable on my sofa.

"I don't mind as long as I'm not in it," I said.

He glanced at the front cover, going quiet as he read the first paragraph. "Ah."

I shook my head. "No way. I can't be in it!"

"Well, it's not really you, it's this woman. Jane."

I snatched it out of his grasp, my jaws already clamping together. My eyes popped out of my head as I studied the caption.

"I'll kill her!" I snarled, throwing the paper on the floor and marching to the front door.

"Tom, wait up! Where are you going? You can't go out like that, even I can see your cock."

I looked down at my joggers. "No, you can't."

"Yes, I can. When you stand up to the light, they're almost see-through. What made you pick up a white pair that are so flimsy?"

"Hell." I dragged them down to my ankles, kicked them off and stalked into my bedroom. "I was wearing these last night! She probably thought I was showing my goods on purpose."

"God Tom, you weren't joking when you said someone hit you with a cricket bat. Looking at your plums." Harry chuckled.

"It wasn't someone. It was me hitting the pommel as Excalibur galloped off to save Jane. Her horse bolted," I said, donning a pair of boxers and some black jogging bottoms. I grabbed a t-shirt from my drawer and went to nab a pair of trainers from a cupboard in the hallway.

"Did she need saving?" Harry asked, a quizzical expression on his face.

I threw him a filthy look. "No, not as it turned out."

Harry bent double, tears streaking from his eyes. "Oh Tom, I like this girl already!"

"So do I," I muttered, striding to the door. Drago hopped out from Harry's side and picked up his lead.

"Where are you going?"

"To Jane's. She's going to be devastated when she sees that." I pointed towards the newspaper.

My phone rang as I took hold of the door.

"Hey, Tom, your phone!" He met me halfway, wiping

tears from his eyes. "So, you're human after all."

"Ha ha, you're so funny," I said to him as I answered the call on my way out, Drago following at my heels.

"Tom, have you seen the papers?" Rick asked.

I gritted my teeth. Nipping back in, I grabbed a baseball cap off the side and said, "Yeah, I'm just leaving now to see Jane."

"What do you mean? You're not going to see the Beast, the Creature from the Black Lagoon, the Swamp Thing, or whatever the tabloids are calling this girl, are you?"

I slammed the door and strode across the lobby. "What business is it of yours, Rick?"

"You agreed to hang out with a babe, Tom. Lots of beautiful Belle's, not the Beast. You can't afford to hang out with an ugly duckling. It will do no end of damage to your sex appeal. And you know what that means."

"What does it mean, Rick? Because I don't see how it's anyone's business than my own who I go out with," I said, thumping my finger onto the security panel. The door popped open, and I strode out onto the pavement. Drago trotted along beside me, trying to keep up. I dumped the hat on my head and pursed my lips. Why were people always dawdling along and getting in my way? Why couldn't they walk in a straight line with a set purpose instead of weaving all over the place as if they were a dropped bag of children's marbles?

"Well, it's all about marketability, Tom. Moving in the right circles, maintaining the correct image – keeping your sponsors happy."

I ground to a halt. "I thought I was an actor, not some prized cow," I said. My jaw ached from grinding my teeth.

"Bull, Tom."

I waved a hand dismissively as a Japanese man with a plethora of cameras around his neck broke away from a diminutive woman and tugged on my arm. I looked down at him and stiffened.

"We like dog. We can have picture?" he said, then turned and chattered like a sparrow to the woman in Japanese. They bowed repetitively, smiling as if they were posing for a wedding photo. I frowned down at him, amazed anyone had the nerve to walk up to me and interrupt when I was on the phone. Then I noticed, 'I love London' and 'Beefeaters do it in furs' badge on his collar. "Tourists?" I asked, pointing at the map in their hands.

"Hai," the man replied beaming, and bowing like a nodding dog in the back of a car.

I considered walking away, but then said loudly, "Of course you can have a picture!" I nodded at the couple and then back to Rick. "Got to go. Fans waiting for a photograph." I smirked slyly and disconnected the call, then rammed my phone into my pocket.

After Drago's photo session, we cut across the park and made our way to Jane's flat. Perhaps he was right, but what happened to all the supposed tolerance we now have in the world? Accepting people for who they are, not what colour skin they have, or if they're disabled or autistic. Or whether they like brown bread instead of white. So why didn't that apply to me? I'm no different from anyone else. I can't plan who I like or love, or why. And what's so remarkable about Jane? Nothing, to the public's eye. And that was the problem. She's just as ordinary as everyone else. She wasn't special because she wasn't beautiful, and the masses believe beautiful people should stick together or it just wasn't cricket? Trouble was, no one knew her well enough to realise it was me who fell short in the beauty stakes, because Jane was far more beautiful on the inside than I am.

As I arrived at her apartment, I glanced up at her window, imagining what she was doing in there and wondering why she had left without waking me. She'd obviously been the one to cover me with a blanket. So, I guess that meant she cared? Or didn't she want to face me first thing in the morning? Did I have morning breath? Or maybe I snored? Talked in my sleep? Farted? Maybe she thought I'd want to get naked? I frowned. I was already mostly there, but Jane was fully clothed. Oh, hell, why did I have to think about that? I looked down at Drago as he turned his head to one side. And it reminded me of Jane's expression last night. God, the odd things that enter your head.

I rang the buzzer and waited.

"Hello?" the female replied. I guessed it was Jane's plump friend, Sarah, Sandie, or whatever?

"Hi, it's Tom. Is Jane there?"

The line went silent. After a few moments, I pressed the button again. Then walked away, looking for a stone to throw up to the window. Why was Jane hiding from me? What had I done wrong? Just as I was about to lob a stone up at the glass, the voice asked, "Tom who?"

"Oh, for fuck's sake!" I heard in the background.

There was a scrabbling sound and then the female voice said, "Shut up, Hunter! How do I know which Tom this is?"

"Really? Because we know hundreds of Toms, don't we, you silly mare!" Hunter hissed.

"It's Tom Austin," I said, glancing at Drago, who had his tongue lolling out of his mouth.

"Tom Austin, as in the actor? Ow! Hunter, take your hand off my…" The conversation was cut short by a loud buzz and a click as the door lock opened.

As I made my way in, I heard the two arguing away. They must have forgotten to disconnect the line.

"Let me handle this Susie, knowing you you'll say something stupid to him and Beth won't see him again."

"And you won't? God, Hunter, you're so conceited sometimes! Mr Bloody Perfect. What's he doing hanging around her, anyway?" I heard Susie reply.

"Fuck! You silly…"

The line went dead as they realised they hadn't disconnected the call. I trotted up the stairs and just as I approached the door; I heard a thumping sound. It appeared there was a wrestling match going on behind the closed door, and as it opened, it surprised me to find the dumpy woman with her hand on the latch.

A frown on her face as she stared at me. "Tom Austin?" she said, her mouth dropping open.

For a moment we both stared at each other, me waiting for her to say more, but she had frozen to the spot as if she was a mannequin. Hunter barged her out of the way, and I fully expected her to tip over as though she were made of plastic.

"Hi Tom," Hunter said jovially. "Would you like to come in?"

Susie shook herself and smiled. At least, I thought it was a smile. It resembled something from the crypt, but I thought that was her intention. "Tea, coffee, tap water, rubdown? He he! Freudian slip. Ha ha!" she said.

I blinked slowly, glancing between her stiff expression and out reaching hands, to Hunter's rolling eyes and hand on his hip. "Ignore her. She's never met anyone famous before."

I nodded, not sure how to respond, and gave the woman a sideways glance.

"Susie sit," Hunter said in a commanding tone far more masculine than I'd heard him before.

Susie and Drago both sat. He, at my feet, and her on the sofa.

"Is Jane here? Did she get home alright?" I ran a hand over my chin. "I mean, did she get home from mine okay? She left. Why did she do that?"

Hunter led me over to a chair by the window and sat me down. Taking a seat, he grimaced. "Women are all mad. Okay, not mad, but they don't think like we do. Not even close."

I leaned forward in my seat as though Hunter was the font of all knowledge and I, a mere pupil. Which was crazy. I mean, I'd dated hundreds of women and here I was listening to the advice of a gay drag queen.

Hunter patted Drago's head as the traitor laid it on his knee. For the first time, I noticed he was dressed in jeans and a t-shirt, catalogue ready to strike a pose. The bloke was a chameleon; I thought randomly as I returned my focus to his words.

"Behind Beth's shell is a kind, tender heart. A beautiful soul. One that's been battered over the years. And just like any mollusc, she has a soft body, which her bruised ego believes is as soft and squidgy and as unattractive as a snail. Are you following me?"

I nodded, but didn't know why. I think it was because I thought I'd just stepped into the funny farm and my best chance of escape was to go along with the lunatics.

"You've seen Jane this morning, then?" I asked.

"Oh yes, but she went out with Karen a little while ago. I think there're bridges to be built there. Wise to give them a little space, if you know what I mean?"

"The letter I was supposed to have been given?"

"Yeah, lord knows why she never gave it to you?" Hunter narrowed his eyes. "Is there a specific reason you came round? Did something happen last night? I presume she was around yours, since she texted me you were playing video games. Did she crush you? Because that woman is crazy good at them."

"I won once," I said, puffing out my chest.

"You beat her?" Hunter shook his head, clearly impressed, and my heart swelled with pride. "I've never known anyone to beat her. She's awesome, I mean pinball wizard, genius."

I narrowed my eyes. "Do you think she let me win?"

"You hurried around here pretty sharp. She said you were zonked out when she left. Is there something the matter?"

Have you ever felt that sudden whiplash when someone changes the subject quickly? Because I was convinced Hunter just skated over my last question. Then I thought back to the headline and grimace. "Have you seen the newspaper yet?"

"No, why? Should we have, because normally none of us show up in any rag?"

I sat for a moment contemplating how I should break this to Jane's best friend.

"Well, I think there was an ulterior motive for Alisha taking Jane's ride yesterday."

"What besides sending her tumbling into the mud?"

I bit my lip. This was hard enough. How was I going to tell Jane?

"Go on," Hunter prompted, cracking a knuckle.

I took out my phone with a slight tremble to my hand. Bought up the headline and showed it to him. Continuing to chew my lip, I watched as he widened the image and scrolled down to read the article.

He looked up over the screen and asked, "Are all your exes such manipulative venomous bitches?"

I swallowed hard. "No, thank god. I haven't always been the best judge of character."

"No shit Sherlock." He leaned back in his chair, pushing his hands through his hair. "How serious are you about Beth? Because if you don't come up with the right answer, I'm going to suggest you call off whatever you're playing right now."

I lowered my gaze, trailing a finger over the edge of the table as I thought. "Jane, I mean Beth and I are friends." There's a rustle from the sofa. I paused and held my breath. "But I want more."

"Why, when you could have anyone?" Susie asked in a clear voice.

I looked between the two of them as though the answer would come to me. How could I describe something I didn't fully understand myself?

"I know Jane, Beth isn't the most beautiful woman on the planet." I began.

Susie snorted and Hunter's gaze blazed with fire, making her drop her eyes and her shoulders slump.

"Go on," Hunter said.

There I was, stood on the edge of a plank, watching the sharks circle below. Sure that any second one would jump up and snatch a limb and drag me into the depths.

I shrugged my shoulders, holding my hands to the ceiling. "I don't know, okay? I can't explain it to you."

"Try," Hunter said.

I picked at a small imperfection on the surface of the veneer. "When Jane's around, I feel as though I'm in a warm bath, and at the same time as if I'm on a runaway train." Hunter nodded, so I continued, "When she touches me, I want her to engulf me. Not just on the outside, but the inside too." I shook my head, convinced I sounded like a crazy fool. "She leaves me breathless, and awkward but with a stupid smile on my face. I want her approval. I want to see that dimple appear and the twinkle in her eyes when she's teasing me. Basically, I want her in my life. Because no matter what happens, good or bad, it's so much better when she's with me."

"Bravo, outstanding performance. Which film did you pinch those lines from?" Susie asked, her face tight, scorn pouring from every inch.

Hunter looked at his phone screen, then said, "Karen's just left the café. If you hurry, you should be able to catch her. She's at the little one on the corner of the road with the blue awning, opposite the park. Let's hope she hears about the headlines from you and not from a street vendor." He pointed to the screen of my phone now sat on the table.

CHAPTER 32

BETH

The instant I walked through my front door; my phone rang. My heart hammered against my chest. Had he awoken and rang me, wondering why I'd left him? Then I saw it was Karen's name, and I took a deep breath. Did I want to hear from her now? Could I stomach her apology or explanation? Perhaps she shared the same view as Susie, that I was wasting my time hoping that Tom would see something in me that no one else did?

At the last minute, I swiped the green button. "Hello?"

"Oh Darling, it's so good to hear you voice! I've so missed you and I have so much to tell you."

"Okay," I said cautiously, chewing half-heartedly on a fingernail.

The silence stretched. "Alright, I owe you an explanation. Meet me at that quaint little café in ten minutes."

I rolled my eyes; it was typical of Karen to stroll into my life after six months of hearing barely anything and expect me to be free at the drop of a hat.

"Oh, come on, you can't tell me you're busy. You

never are on a Sunday morning at this time."

"A lot can happen in six months," I said. It was on the tip of my tongue to say I'd just got in from Tom's, but I would not give her that titbit of information after the bunny episode. Then there was the other part of me that was kicking myself for leaving him in the first place. Was I mental not to throw myself at him? Especially as he'd groaned my name as I moved away from his body. Much as I loved every moment with him, the thought that someone would jump out and cry, 'surprise, you've been caught on camera' any second and expect me to laugh at my humiliation prevented me from truly believing it was real. What happened if Tom was only getting a kick out of taunting the ugly girl? It seemed more likely than he thought I was dateable, desirable, beddable.

"I really have missed you, Beth. I know I've made mistakes and I'm a horrible person, but without you in my life, who else is going to keep me on the straight and narrow? Besides, I want you to be my bridesmaid!"

"Bridesmaid! The Monaco guy?" I wet my lips. This was too much of a temptation to miss out on.

"Meet me in five minutes. I've got us a table overlooking the green and have just ordered you a breakfast tea with a warm croissant and raspberry jam."

My stomach groaned. "Evil tempestuous!" I moaned. "Alright, I'll be there in five, and no comments about my appearance."

"As if I would."

***

I could see Karen well before I got to the café. Two waiters hovered over the woman I considered a witch, decked out in blues and greens and striking as a peacock. I strolled along as unnoticeable as a peahen, in my jeans and taupe top with a bulky over coat. Since leaving Tom's, I couldn't shake the chill that settled around my heart and penetrated my bones.

"Beth darling!" Karen said, beaming at me as if nothing had changed between us.

My mouth twisted, and the waiter took one look at me and scarpered. I looked at her hard and she smiled, a slight glint in her eyes and my heart softened.

"You look well," I said, bending down to place a kiss on her cheek as I slid into the seat beside her. However hard I tried; I couldn't stay mad at Karen. So many times, she'd been there for me over the years, the big sister that I'd never had.

"You haven't changed." She smirked, dashing a tear from her eye with a manicured fingernail.

I nodded, waiting for the follow up.

"Literally, haven't changed." She winked as I threw my handbag on the chair beside me and took a slurp of tea.

"Ha ha, neither have you. No one's thrown a bucket of water over you yet. Shame."

Her mouth curved up, and she chuckled. Leaning forward, she wrapped me in her arms and sighed. "God, I've missed you, I've had no one to fence with."

"I missed you too." I added grudgingly. "Lord only knows why; the Emerald City has been happier without you."

"Has it?" Her eyes searched mine.

"Yes and no," I said honestly. "I am glad to see you. Even though you're a rubbish postwoman."

"Ah yes, your letter to Tom. I'm sorry about that. I was in a bad place when that happened." Her eyes teared up, and she put on her sunglasses. "I don't expect you to forgive me, but I hope you'll understand?" She paused. I waited, hugging my cup in my hands. "Toby, the man who I stayed with in Monaco. The man I believed was the love of my life." She took out a delicate handkerchief and dabbed ineffectively at her cheek. "Well, the first day I was back on set after breaking my arm, he called to say all the plans we'd made were on hold. He was returning to Hollywood to direct this stupid movie. Instead of our life beginning in a month, it would be at least a year! I was so sick of waiting for him, when all he did was move the goal posts." Her hands fluttered as tears continued to pour. "I'm sorry Jane, I took one look at Tom's face, filled with disappointment it was me and not you. Then I just snapped, and when he didn't say a word about knowing all about Toby's decision to return to the film industry. Well, I... I saw red - and green. Tom was starring in Guy Fawkes, the film Toby was directing, and I forgot all about you. I was just so mad at the men in my life!" She balled up the sodden rag and tightened her mouth. "And I honestly thought it wouldn't hurt you because a man like Tom Austin couldn't really be interested..." She caught her breath.

"In me," I finished for her.

She leaned forward and grasped my hand. "I'm so sorry, darling! I shouldn't have done any of it. You're beautiful, but guys like Toby and Tom are all the same. It's so easy for them to make a girl fall in love with them and then cast them off like yesterday's mail. They don't care about the pieces they leave behind."

I pursed my lips. "That might be true for Toby, Karen, but that's not Tom. He's been such a good friend to me."

"Oh, I don't doubt he'd be a good friend, but that doesn't make him a great boyfriend. At least, not for a girl like you."

My eyes flared. How dare she say such a thing about me, as if no one could love me.

"Don't look at me like that Beth. I only meant girls like you who don't sleep around. You're a girl to take home to their mother, to bear their children. You're not a lover, you're a wife. Not a good-time girl like I was."

"So, you've changed?" I asked sharply.

"Well, I'm getting married. Settling down Beth. I thought you'd be pleased for me?" she pouted.

I pushed my hands into my pockets. "So, you've made it up with Toby? Is that why you went to America, to work things out?"

"Initially, yes, but he was always busy, and that's when I met Charles, who had all the time in the world for me. When he proposed, I said yes. We're marrying next month. Isn't that wonderful?"

I fought hard not to roll my eyes. Looking across to the park, I watched as lovers strolled hand in hand. Could anyone get over 'the love of their life' and fall in love with another in such a short time frame? I knew I couldn't, but could Karen? "Let me get this straight," I said, bringing my gaze back to hers. "In the last six months, you've tried to work it out with Toby. Failed. Met Charles had a whirlwind romance and got engaged to be married?" I glanced at the enormous diamond on her finger. "And the wedding's in a month's time?"

"Yes, isn't it wonderful?"

There was that phrase again; wonderful. Was it wonderful, or was she trying too hard to convince herself? I watched the ring glitter in the sunlight and wondered what had dazzled her most. Charles, or the enormous lump of fossilised carbon on her finger.

"So, you're over Toby?"

She looked down at her hand, twisting the rock one way, then another. "Toby who?" she said, not meeting my eyes.

"As long as you're one hundred percent sure you want this, then I'm happy for you," I said, grasping her hand in mine and giving it a squeeze. "But if you're not..." I left it hanging. She knew what I meant.

"Everything will be fine," she said. The words sounded hollow even to my ears.

"Yes, I'm sure it will. Everything seems sparkly when it's brand new," I said, placing my thumb over the gem. "It's only with time it becomes tarnished."

Shortly after, she handed me a tattered blue envelope adorned with bunnies and with a sad little smile, made her excuses, and left. I was glad we were on friendly terms again, but a gnawing headache had started up over one eye when I thought of her forthcoming nuptials.

CHAPTER 33

TOM

Striding along the pavement, Drago by my side, a jumble of thoughts collided in my mind and none of them made me any less sure who had the rudder on the ship I was sailing. Every time a new feeling took up residence in my body, heart, soul, or wherever feelings lived, a stronger or more intense one took its place.

When I first met Jane, I'd forgotten her name seconds after I'd heard it. Dismissing her as I would a cog in a clock. Then gradually things shifted, in the same way as the sea meanders over the shore until it engulfs it. Threading its way through tufts of sea grass and settling there to become a part of the landscape, Jane had become part of my life.

I glanced over at the park. Spotting movement in the trees, three small brown birds flitted through the branches. They were sparrows. Strange how I'd never realised how interesting and detailed they were before.

Then I saw her, a frown etched on her forehead. My heart did a kerplunk and then spiked up and down like a seismograph tracking an earthquake.

"Jane," I said.

She jumped, a smile replacing the frown for an instant before a tightness came into her features.

"Oh, hello Tom. Fancy seeing you here." She patted Drago, and he sat down by her feet.

"It was intentional. I came as soon as I saw... You weren't there when I awoke. Is everything all right? You look pensive. Hunter said you'd met Karen?"

"Yes, I did, but she had to dash off." She picked up a cup in front of her, looked at it and then put it down again.

I sat down. "Do you mind?" I asked, resting my hands on the table.

She smiled. "You're already sitting, Mr Rochester."

"I can get up again if you want some space?" I said, a hand on the back of the chair.

"No, no. I'm only teasing! I don't need the space."

"Ah, that's alright then. Did everything go well between you and Karen? You looked caught up in your thoughts when I approached?"

"If you're needling to see if we made up, the answer is yes. All's good in the world of Beth and Karen. Although she landed a bombshell – she's getting married next month."

I lifted my eyebrows. "That's good news, isn't it? I haven't spoken to Toby lately, but I guess he's finally did the decent thing."

She shook her head. "Not to Toby."

"Not to Toby?" I repeated with a slight toss of my

head. "But when I was out there, they were going strong. Everything appeared to be hearts and flowers. What happened?"

"Charles and a five-carat diamond ring. Oh, I don't suppose it was just the diamond ring that swayed it. She said she's fed up waiting for him."

"Wow." I couldn't think of anything else to say.

"Still, I'm sure they'll work it out. Was there a reason to come and find me or were you just in desperate need of my company?" she asked. The faint smile dropped from her face. "Oh, what's happened? Unless you're acting right now, I'd say we have a funeral to attend."

I ground my teeth together. "It's a possibility."

"Should it worry me who's funeral it is?" Her brow crinkled. "We're not talking about a family member or friend, are we?"

"No, Alisha's, if I ever get hold of her. I swear if she walked by this minute, I could happily wring her neck."

Jane picked up her phone and tapped on the screen to check the news. Her face paled as she studied the headlines.

"Oh, you can't say she doesn't have impeccable timing, can you?" she said as she took hold of my hand and gave it a squeeze. The gesture, so typical of Jane, ignited a furnace in me. I pulled my hand away from hers and slammed it against the table.

"Goddamn it, Jane, why does she keep doing this to us?"

"Us?" A ghost of a whisper left her mouth.

I took hold of her hand, felt a slight tremor, and brought it to my lips. "Yes. This affects both of us." I met her eyes, saw the confusion, and took a breath. "Why did you leave this morning? It wasn't the headlines, so…?"

Just then, my phone rang. I looked at the screen and laid it on the table.

Jane glanced at it and said, "Answer it, Tom. He's probably worried."

"Blow St John, it has nothing to do with him."

"He rung me a couple of times when I was talking to Karen, but I didn't pick up. He's your friend. You should answer him."

I narrowed my eyes and then snatched up the phone. Punched at the green button and growled. "Rivers, what do you want?" Jane gave me a look, and I tempered my reply. "Sorry, it's been a stressful morning."

"Tom, I saw the papers and had to ring. Have you seen Beth? Is she alright?" I glanced over. She sat on the edge of her seat with her head cocked to one side.

"Wherever she is, I'm sure she's fine," I said.

Her eyes widened. 'Tom!' she mouthed. 'What are you doing?'

"Don't tell me you haven't seen her?" Rivers said. "I've been trying to ring her ever since I saw the headline. This could be serious, Tom. I thought you liked this girl? How can it not concern you?"

Jane reached for my phone, but I wrestled it away from her grasp. "Hold on to your breeches, old man. Jane's here with me now and she's fine."

"Put her on the line if she's with you, and for god's sake, call her by her name!"

"Jane is her name," I said stubbornly.

"Her real name." He insisted.

Jane took the phone from my hand, and I watched as her face lit up. A vein throbbed in my temple, and I reminded myself to relax my jaw as an ache started up under my ear.

"Rivers, I'm so sorry I missed your calls. It's been a busy morning," she said.

"That's alright darling. As long as you're okay. Is Tom looking after you? Did you see the papers this morning or was Rochester the bringer of bad news?"

She chuckled lightly. Now there were two people on my list I wanted to throttle. What the hell was he doing with her phone number, anyway? As I sat like a gooseberry, watching them converse, the world around me darkened and I looked up to see if a cloud had shrouded the sun. I squinted and brought my attention back to hers. She sat there looking at me with a little frown between her brows, my phone in her hand, outstretched, ready for me to take it. I snatched it from her grasp and stared back at her.

"What?" I asked.

My question seemed to amuse her, as the Mona Lisa smile found its way onto her face.

"How does he have your number, anyway?" Then I added lamely. "And what gives him the right to call me Rochester?"

"Tea?" she asked, looking towards a waiter.

"What?"

"Would you like a drink to help you calm down?"

"I'll need something stronger than tea," I muttered as the waiter approached.

Jane's smile deepened. "A pot of tea for two, please." She glanced at me. "And a pastry. The one with the caramel sauce and almonds on top."

I licked my lips and tried to ignore the rumble in my stomach.

The man nodded, smiling at her. "I'll be back in a minute," he said. Throwing a look at me over his shoulder, I watched recognition dawn and glared at him until he turned and hurried away.

"I don't need feeding Jane."

"I beg to differ," she said. I glared at her. "You can work it off."

This was promising. "How?" I asked, smiling wolfishly. Her cheeks flared, and I laughed. Thank God, I never put jeans on. The thought of working it off with Jane had my engine revving; pistons pumped, fuel flooding through my system and my tick over rate on the high side.

The waiter arrived with our drinks and my pastry. He hovered, stepping from foot to foot.

"I hope everything is alright for you? Er, do you think I could have your autograph?" He played with a monogrammed napkin in his hand. "I'm a big fan of yours."

I took it from him and scrawled my signature across it.

I expected him to scurry away, but he caught Jane's eye. "Er, do you think I could have yours too, miss?" he asked.

"Oh, I'm not famous," Jane said, smiling at him.

"But you are. I've seen you in the papers. You're much prettier in real life."

She looked at me, and a dimple appeared. "Why not?" she said, taking the napkin from him.

I picked up the pastry and ate thoughtfully. She seemed to take a long time to write her name, but I couldn't see what she wrote, with the teapot in the way. And after a mouthful or two of the almond plait, I closed my eyes and savoured the taste.

"Looks like you're enjoying that, Mr Rochester?"

I opened my eyes to find we were alone and brushed a few crumbs from my lips.

"Oh yeah, I think all my Christmases have come at once. I can't remember the last time I had one of these."

"They're good, aren't they?" She smirked, looking flushed.

I nodded, taking another bite. "What did you write on his napkin?"

"Well, I was spoilt for choice. So, in the end I just wrote 'Love your buns, the Beast of Bermondsey aka Swamp thing' and drew a beast rising from a puddle. Thought that was a nice touch."

My mouth hung open.

"Well, he wouldn't have had a clue who Elizabeth Bennet was. I thought I might as well embrace the whole beast thing. Can't beat them. Might as well join them." She shrugged.

"Your name's Elizabeth?" was the only thing I could think to say when the thing I wanted to do was kiss her.

CHAPTER 34

BETH

I studied a piece of pastry dangling from Tom's lip and mentally wrestled my tongue not to stick out and snake its way to his mouth to lick off the morsel. I've never wanted to give someone mouth to mouth so badly in my life. I was salivating just at the thought of engulfing his lips with mine. Instead, I reached forth with my thumb and brushed the crumb away. Dragging the pad lovingly over his plump lower lip.

His gaze intensified, and I found it impossible to look away. He'll crush your heart, my brain screamed, hitting the panic button. I took my hand away as if someone had tickled under my armpit.

Waking up, I said, "Yes, my name's Elizabeth Jane Bennet. It's nice to be formally acquainted, Mr Tom Austin."

"Herm, if we're doing formal, my name is actually Thomas Edward Austin. Tea for short."

I choked on my tea, ironically, and flatteringly it ran from my nose as I scrambled to grab a napkin.

Tom laughed, a deep rumbling sound that made my insides flutter, and looked around him. "No one's taking a picture of you, are they? I can just imagine the headlines tomorrow!"

"Return of the slime ball, snot monster makes a play for Hollywood hunk," I said, blowing my nose on a tissue I'd found in my pocket.

Tom stilled. "Is that what you're doing, Jane, making a play for me?"

"Oh crikey, no. No way! Never in a month of Sundays." I laughed, but it sounded thin and tinny to me.

The smile on his face dropped. "Is that because you like Rivers better than me? He has your number, and you've only met him once."

I bit my lip. "He asked for it and I didn't see any harm in giving it to him."

I watched as his mouth tightened.

"It wasn't because I liked him more than you."

He gave me a sceptical look.

I threw up my hands. "This is ridiculous. No one like Rivers is going to ask me out any more than you will. For five years I can count on one hand how many guys have been interested in me. Do you know how many there are? Exactly zero, nil, nada. No one since Josh left me, and he wasn't that enamoured. He wouldn't take me out without the full works, and it was always 'Beth, you should have a boob job, and have you been stuffing the cakes again, looking at your thighs you…'" I trailed off. What guy wanted to hear from a moaning Minnie? I dropped my head and looked at my hands.

"Jane, look at me," he commanded.

"I'm sorry. I shouldn't have gone on. Can we still be friends?" I cringed. Now I was pathetic and plain! A winning combination if there ever was one.

"Jane. Elizabeth Jane Bennet, look at my face," he said.

Gradually, I lifted my head. His voice was hard, and I didn't want to see the anger and judgement in his eyes, but as much as I didn't want to see the truth, I wouldn't hide from it either.

"This is me. Not the actor playing a part, reading from a script. It is me being truthful and as brutally honest as I can be. You're not beautiful, not in the superficial way. Not in the classical way, to grace the cover of a magazine."

"You're like that sparrow over there. Blending in with the branches and twigs. Not immediately jumping up and smacking you in the face with how dazzling their plumage is, but when you look closer, you see it's not just a plain brown bird. It possesses many tones of brown, each as individual and striking as the other."

"And what is that little bird doing? It's busy feeding its young, taking the ants and aphids from the tree, so that both it and the babies will flourish. You're like that bird to me, Jane."

I grinned through my tears. "Thank you, Tom. I've never been called a sparrow before." I gulped.

He took a man-sized tissue from his pocket. "Here, use this. And you'd better make sure you get that booger hanging from your nose."

My eyes widened in horror, and I wished I was one of

those women who carried a compact around with them. I had at one time, but not since Josh and I broke up. "Has it gone?" I asked, unwilling to show him my nostrils.

"I was only pulling your leg. Your nose is lovely."

I narrowed my eyes. "I bet Alisha never had snot hanging from her nose."

"No, but then, when you're a malicious android, you wouldn't, would you? Anyway, you look cute with a rosy nose."

"Thanks." I chuckled. "I feel better already."

"Anyway, if it wasn't for me marking my territory everywhere I went, Rivers would have made a play for you. I've even confused Drago by peeing up too many lampposts!"

"I don't believe that, but thanks anyway. You make me laugh." I reached down and stroked Drago's coat. When I looked up again, Tom was watching me, a sober look on his face. He reached over and cupped my face, running the pad of his thumb over my cheek.

"It's not all a joke, Beth. I seriously want to take you out. Not as a friend or a colleague, or whatever foolish thing your mind is telling you. I want to take you out on a date with candlelight and music and wine."

"But you don't drink…"

"Shush, Elizabeth Jane Bennet."

He leaned forward and kissed me. And for a moment there was only him and me, with a dizzying number of firecrackers going off all over my body. My heart took over from my head and I let it take flight.

Then, aware of a shadow, our eyes cracked open to find the waiter standing with his phone in his hands as if he was taking a picture.

"Tomorrow's news?" he said cheekily.

"Don't you dare!" we both said in unison. And then laughed, hopeful that this was the start of something new.

Although for me it was more than a little daunting, but I was ready to take the risk this time. To trust another man with my heart, perhaps my body, and if my brain was still silently screaming at me – well, for now, I'd locked it in a box and partially turned the key.

The End

Book 2 tells the story of how Elizabeth Jane Bennet aka Plain Jane and Thomas Edward Austin or (Tea for short) aka Mr Rochester's romance progresses. Of course, with Jane, nothing is ever straightforward and easy or lacking humour. Here's a taste of book two...

PLAIN JANE - SEXY BEAST

By Rebecca Rayne

CHAPTER 1

BETH

Whoever thought the Beast, the Swamp thing or the Creature from the Black Lagoon would have a date tonight with the hottest hunk in Hollywood, heartthrob Tom Austin? I know you're probably wondering why this gorgeous actor would even consider going out with such a monster. Although this monster wasn't as bad as you might think, because this gruesome creature was none other than me, Elizabeth Jane Bennet, a thirty-one-year-old makeup artist from Bermondsey. That's a fanciful embellishment. I'm not actually from Bermondsey, but it fitted at the time. My aliases, the brainchild of Tom's ex-girlfriend, and plastered across the tabloids with fantastical pictures of me in muddy puddles and crumpled up in a heap after Tom knocked me off my bike. Okay, they weren't that fantastical. Just me, an ordinary woman, slightly camera shy, shown in her worst light.

I'd left Tom after a leisurely walk around the park with his Leopard hound, Drago, and dashed up the stairs to my apartment, my feet light and my heart all a quiver. As I burst through the door, Hunter, the gorgeous drag queen, who was fast superseding Susie, my other roommate, as my best friend, pounced on me.

"Hey Beth, what happened?"

"I've got a date," I said, taking hold of Hunter's hands and jumping up and down.

"Really, who with?" a voice asked dryly.

I shot a look towards the sofa; unaware anyone was on it. "Susie?" I asked.

Her head popped up, and she furrowed her brow. "The spiel pretty boy Tom gave you didn't draw you in, did it? Tell me you've got more sense than that?" She took one look at my face and rolled her eyes, then disappeared back behind the sofa.

"Ignore her. Sour old sow," Hunter said.

"I am not!" Susie replied, hotly.

"PMS," Hunter whispered as we ceased our jumping.

"I heard that," she said from behind the sofa. "I'm just looking out for Beth's best interests. Dating an actor is a terrible idea. You can't trust anything that comes out of their mouths, and they're always screwing their co-stars." Susie reasoned.

"That's painting everyone in the acting profession with a wide brush, you cynical old cow." Hunter let go of my hands and walked over to the sofa, hands on his hips. "Why can't you be happy for her? You're her second-best friend, you're supposed to support her. Not lie there like the grim reaper – pissing on her parade." Hunter's eyes flashed.

"I'm not old and I'm her best friend. You, Mr Fakery, are her flatmate. Nothing more."

"Still sore about me calling you fat, Susie? I thought

you'd have got over that by now. Guess not. Truth hurts, sister."

"Why don't you go earn some money shagging that poisoned dwarf you keep chasing?" Susie's tone cut through the air like a knife. I winced and walked over to them.

"Hey guys, we're all friends here. There's no need for this. You know I love you both and I hate to see you at each other's throats."

"Seriously Beth, I'm not getting that close to him." She hooked a finger at Hunter. "He's a prime example not to go out with someone who thinks they're god's gift!"

"I'd just like to say I love you too, Beth." Hunter smirked.

"Oh, for god's sake, you pathetic excuse for a man," Susie hissed.

I ran my fingers through my hair. "Stop, the pair of you. You're behaving like two-year-olds! Whatever grudge you've got with each other, it's time to bury it – deep." I was just about to say more when my phone rang. My heart jolted and then, after I'd looked at the screen and realised it wasn't Tom, returned to its normal rhythm. "I'll take this in my room. Play nicely, please." I walked away, but before I turned my back, they were back to griping at each other. I rolled my eyes. Could this really be over the argument they had months ago?

I closed the door to my bedroom and tapped on the call. "Eve, is everything alright?" Eve Sharp was my boss. She ran the makeup department at the studios where Tom starred in the series Ironclaw.

Filming was due to start on the third series in a fortnight, so it was all hands on deck to get the makeup and costumes ready in time. Meetings had run back-to-back for the last week, discussing the new characters and what they would need from the special effects department. Eve was already pulling her hair out at the number of costume and character changes needed for this season, but from what I'd heard, Tom would have the toughest deal of us all. The management team had decided that the storyline needed some ramping up to draw the audience in. I guess they hadn't witnessed last episode's filming schedule, and they obviously weren't looking at all the injuries Tom sustained.

Perhaps they'd hire a stuntman this time? I hoped they'd make their star take it easy and pass off the stunts to the professionals, but the stubborn son of a gun would probably insist he'd do the least dangerous ones himself.

"Oh, Beth Darling, you have no idea what a week I've had. I'm ready for a stiff gin and a visit to my colourist. I swear this week's been so stressful I've doubled the amount of grey I've got!"

"Anything I can help with?"

"God, I hate to ask, but I'm just going to dive in and say it. I need you to go on a trip. Hope it will do you a favour as I see you've hit the headlines again. Was it that awful ex of Tom's again? She really has it in for you, doesn't she? I wonder why? Another unflattering picture of you, too!"

"Yes, well, what was the reason for your call?" I furrowed my brow. It wasn't like Eve to witter, she was a straight to the point with a sharp needle kind of woman, just like her name.

She tittered, and a chill raced down my spine. "I know this is short notice, but would you be a darling and go to Paris to do Demais' face for me?"

"Demais? The model? When?" I couldn't hide the excitement in my voice. Demais was as popular as electric cars in the fashion and film world. Everyone wanted one, and had to have one, but couldn't afford it.

"That's the problem. It's today darling. For a week. Do you think you could? I'm desperate here. Please, darling, this could make your name internationally. Please say you can."

I must have groaned. Or made some other sounds that I felt but was sure I hadn't voiced, because she threw more and more incentives into the mix. By the time she took a breath, I was crumbling under the weight. Like an Olympic medallist ladened with gold, ribbons and flowers, then she added a cuddly toy for good measure.

As soon as I got off the phone to Eve, I called Tom. Our first date would have been tonight, only that was blown out of the water by Eve and pressing work commitments. My heart ached, but I didn't want to let Eve down. She'd helped me so much. I owed her this small favour after she'd got me the job at London fashion week and introduced me to famous photographers.

When it went to voicemail, I left this message: "Tom, I'm so sorry, but I have to let you down tonight. Eve's in desperate need of a favour, so I've agreed to help her out. Please understand. I'm flying to Paris... now, but I'll ring you later. I was really looking forward to our date. Hopefully, you'll want to go next week? Bye, your Jane."

I threw everything in my suitcase, called a cab, and raced through the living room past Hunter and Susie, who were still arguing. And thundered down the staircase, a trouser leg hanging from my suitcase, and nearly bowled over a guy hanging around the main entrance. "Sorry!" I called over my shoulder as I wrenched open the back door to the cab and wedge my case behind the driver's seat. I was just about to get in when Hunter stopped me.

"Where are you going?" he asked breathlessly.

"I've got to go to Paris to do Demais' makeup. Wish me luck!"

"Luck? It's me who needs luck. Why is it no one sends me to Paris to do the hottest new models' makeup?"

I shrugged and smiled weakly. "I'll miss you, Hunter. Take care."

He sighed dramatically, "I'll miss you too. But I'm not thrilled you're leaving me alone with Miss moody breeches."

"Make your peace," I said, kissing him on the cheek.

He mimicked hitting someone over the head with a shovel and grinned. "What about your hot date?" he asked as I got in the cab.

"I've had to postpone it," I said through the partially opened window, while I clutched my handbag to my chest and watched Hunter's gloomy face transform into a leering grin.

"I guess I'll have to console him then," he said.

I crossed my eyes and stuck my tongue out at him.

Although there was a part of me that wanted to beg him to do just that. At least that would keep Alisha away from both of us until I got back.

Last time I hit the news headlines as the Beast, Tom's PR consultant and lawyers managed to keep any journalists from tracking me down and taking a statement. Tom had warned me they probably wouldn't be so successful this time. So being out of the country should help keep my anonymity for a bit longer. Or so I hoped.

As I waited at the airport, my phone rang. I scrambled with my case and handbag to answer it in time.

My heart racing in my chest. "Oh Rivers," I said, scrambling to hand my case to the woman at the check-in desk.

"Did you think I was Tom?" he asked.

I bit my lip. "Yes, sorry if I sounded disappointed. I rang him as soon as I knew I was leaving the country. But he never picked up, and I wanted to make sure he'd get the message as we were going out tonight," I explained.

"You're leaving the country? This isn't anything to do with the papers, is it?"

"No, no. Eve, my boss has an emergency. So, I'm flying to Paris to take over from one of her staff who's ill. Nothing as exciting as fleeing the country because there's a national beast hunt." I chuckled.

"Well, I'm glad that isn't the reason. I feel so responsible Beth. That incident happened on my land. Would you like me to ring Tom and make sure he knows?"

I thought about Tom's reaction to Rivers phoning me last time, and what he would think if he got the message, I'd cancelled via him. "No, that's fine. I've left him a message and I'll call him as soon as I'm settled in. Look Rivers, it was really kind of you to ring, but I'm afraid I have to run. Speak to you later?"

"Sure thing, Beth, as long as you're alright?"

We said our goodbyes and I finished checking in, then made a run for the boarding area.

CHAPTER 2

TOM

By the time Drago and I got back to my apartment, Rick was standing in the foyer pacing back and forth. I lifted an eyebrow as I watched him pace like a caged bear, then race over to me, all hot and sweaty, when I opened the door.

"Are you on a new fitness regime?" I asked him as he panted for breath. His face was as red and dewy as a greenhouse tomato.

"All these newspaper headlines you keep making are going to give me a heart attack!" he said.

I walked past him and put my key in the front door. Drago took more interest in Rick than he normally would after getting his customary treat. I guess he liked the sweaty tomato Rick better than the reek of expensive aftershave one.

"I don't keep making the headlines at all, and neither does Jane. It's Alisha who keeps creating these stories. Why don't you hang around her door and complain about them?"

"She's not my client. And anyway, she'd eat me alive," he said, following me inside.

My jaw ticked as I watched a drop of sweat slide down his nose and hit the floor. "Wait here." I said, loud enough for Drago to hesitate as he padded to his basket. I entered my bedroom, grabbed a hand towel from a cupboard and threw it to Rick and then went through to the lounge and sat down. I was glad to see Harry had tidied up from this morning, I didn't want to explain to Rick why someone had slept on my sofa. The guy was one DNA strand off a bloodhound. He'd sniff around until he got the whole story and then there would be an inquisition. And probably a witch hunt, too. "Alisha doesn't touch anything but prime beef steak, so you'll be safe, mate," I said.

Rick sat down heavily beside me and threw the towel on my oak coffee table as he picked up a game controller. I glared at the towel and was about to toe it onto the floor as though it was a biohazard, when Drago hopped out of his basket, grabbed it and took it back to his bed.

"Want me to get that back for you?" Rick asked as he scrolled down the player menu.

I glanced at Drago as he chanked at the rag and shook my head. "No, it's too late for that. And I'm not sure I wanted it back anyway."

"Wow, look at that score," Rick said as he eyed the leader board. "Have you been playing as Mouse? That's not like you."

"No." From the second I spotted Rick in the foyer, the lightness had dropped away, and my teeth were set on edge, my stomach bubbling. I knew what herald this visit, and I knew I wouldn't like what Rick had to say. For the first time in a very long time, I wished I'd chosen another profession, or hired a different manager. "If you want to play, get on with it."

Rick flicked on his character and set the game in motion. "So, was it one of your brothers who posted that score? Or your sister, I hear she's an outstanding player?"

"No, only Harry's over here. The rest are in the States and Joe's in Germany."

"Oh, so who's Mouse?" he asked casually.

"How should I know? Some online player, I suppose."

Rick chuckled, and I narrowed my eyes. "Ah, so you don't know who this player is? Must be galling when they post such a score and against Beft too?"

I mowed down Rick's character and laid the controller on the table. "Get on with it, Rick. You obviously never came here to discuss video games. So, say what you need to say and leave."

"What's with all the hostility, we used to be friends?" he said.

"Yes, that was before you controlled my private life."

"I don't control your private life, Tom. I advise you on your public persona," he said, turning to me with tightness in his shoulders.

"Go on. Let's hear what you're going to advise me to do with my public persona." I looked into his eyes and watched as his flickered away from mine. I set my jaw.

"You have the launch of Guy Fawkes next month. I've arranged for Adele Adiz to accompany you."

"Why, you've never pimped me out before?"

Rick winced. "I never had to before. You can't seriously want to take this girl? I mean, look at her." He scrolled through the tabloid pictures of Jane on his phone. None of them flattering, and a few that never made the press. I wondered briefly how he got hold of them. Not that it mattered. Rick had drawn his conclusions about her from those few odd pictures, and now he and the company he represented wouldn't stomach her as my date. I was well aware how tight the contract was, and at the time, it never even entered my head to insist on having more control. I never needed it. I'd always dated glamorous women, and never, in my wildest dreams thought I'd be interested in someone like Jane. The thought made my stomach roll. Was I really that shallow? Of course, that wouldn't stop me from seeing her in private, but on public events, Rick had the final say so.

"You can't judge someone by these few unflattering pictures, Rick. No one looks great in these circumstances!"

"No one but you and the uber attractive. This girl doesn't fall into that category, and even if she did, she'd still be fighting an uphill battle. The public's opinion is set."

"This is bloody ridiculous! How am I going to explain that in public I'll have to throw a bag over her head and pretend we're not together?"

"Seriously Tom, you're dating this woman? But why, when you can have the choice of anyone? I certainly wouldn't touch this girl if I looked like you."

I rose from my seat, my fists balled. "And how would you know what you'd do as me, Rick? It's not like you haven't hit your fair share of branches on your way down the ugly tree! Considerably more than Jane has, I might add, and she doesn't sweat like a pig walking a few yards either. So, what gives you the right to judge her?"

I watched as Rick's face blanched, flushed to purple and then settled into its normal ruddy complexion. "This is business Tom. And business says from now on your public persona will be linked to Adele Adiz, not the Beast of Bermondsey." He got up and walked to the door. But I was faster and more agile. I'd overtaken and slipped in front of him, blocking the exit.

"Is that the final say so then?" I asked, "You're going to dictate who I'm seen out in public with?"

"It's only business, Tom. It's nothing personal," he said. "If you want to hang around with some Plain Jane in private, it's your own affair."

"She doesn't deserve your opinion of her Rick."

He reached around me and took hold of the door handle. "I don't care. Another couple of months and you'll have found a younger, more attractive model to bed. You probably won't recall this girl at all. Good managers are worth more than passing fancies. Let's hope you remember that before you say one too many offensive remarks to me and find yourself looking for a new man."

I gripped onto the door tightly. "How much longer is there left on our contract?"

Rick turned around as he reached the outer doorway. "Seven months with a contingency for another two years."

"Consider this as notice of termination. I won't be

renewing your contract when seven months is up. You'll be getting it in writing first thing in the morning."

"Decisions made in haste, repented at leisure. You're live to regret this Austin, mark my words."

"The only regret I have is, I'll have to work with you until that time." I closed the door, puffed out an exasperated breath and called Drago to heel. I grabbed the ragged towel out of his mouth and threw it in the bin on my way out. "Disgusting habit!" I said to him, giving him a stern look. He dropped his head and whimpered. "Yes, you should be ashamed of yourself, consorting with the enemy. What would Jane think, huh?" His ears pricked up, and he walked along jauntily. "Ugh, yes, you're right, she'd forgive you."

Somehow, a smile ended up on my face. Tonight, was our first proper date. I kicked up my heels as I strode along. "I think we'll see if Harry's free for a jog in the park. Do you think that's a top-notch idea boy?" His tongue lolled out of his mouth. "Yes, that's what I thought, too."

Halfway to Harry's, I'd realised I left my phone behind. Behind where, I wasn't sure. I couldn't recall having it since this morning at the café. Blast, what a pain in the arse. Perhaps I'd just ring them later and see if they'd got it. I could collect it tomorrow, rather than return today. I'd pick Jane up at seven, as there was no desperate need to pick it up beforehand.

CHAPTER 3

BETH

Arriving at Paris' Charles de Gauille airport, I trudged my way through customs after collecting my case and found a man in a crumpled suit holding my name up. I thought the French were supposed to be the epitome of style and chic, but this guy looked as though he was auditioning for Columbo? Apparently, he was my driver, or so I discovered as he threw my suitcase into the back of his car as though it was dirty laundry and got in the driver's seat. Jean-Paul, as his name turned out to be, liked to drive with the window down, shouting colourful expletives and waving hand signals at other drivers. If he spoke to me, I barely heard over the hoot of horns and screech of brakes. It took us about an hour to get to my hotel, the constant stop starting and near misses had my knuckles tightening around the seat and my stomach lurching, that when I got out of the cab, I felt as though I'd been in a boxing match. As we got out, he tossed my suitcase to me and said, "You 'ave five minutes, mademoiselle. 'urry, 'urry, they wait for you!"

"What?" I asked the driver.

He rolled his eyes and lit a cigarette, leaning on the side of his taxi. "Se presse, we 'aven't got all day!" He chided, waving his hands at me.

I raised my eyebrows at him and pointed at my chest. "Me?" I looked around as if I was in a crowd.

He puffed on his cigarette as though it was a steam train and dropped it to the ground crushing it underneath his hand stitch leather shoes. I frowned. Did all taxi drivers have such expensive shoes in Paris? And for a second, I thought I'd had a stroke – how could anyone smoke that fast?

"Quel, get a move on. You're 'ear to work, not gawp at de architecture!" He tapped his watch and lit another cigarette.

God, that guy could smoke. I dashed into the hotel and was back out in 7 minutes.

"What took 'ou so long? Merde de English," he said, dropping a fag to join the rest on the pavement.

The smile fell from my face, and I glared at him. Thank God he was only dropping me off. Working with this jerk would have me pulling my hair out by the end of the week.

"Where are you taking me?" I asked as I got back in the car, silently praying it wouldn't be a long journey.

"We 're going tu de Lourve. De studio as a room dere to do Demais' makeup and after de tu beautiful creations will work in 'armony."

"Huh? I beg your pardon?"

Jean-Paul tightened his grip on the wheel, then stuck his head out of the open car window and waved his fist at another motorist. "Imbecile, let your granny drive next time!" He looked over his shoulder at me and said, "Demais will promote de Lourve and de Lourve will 'er. They complement each other, comprendre?"

My eyes widened as a car approached, Jean-Paul's head snapped back to the road, and he wrenched the wheel, narrowly avoiding the vehicle. I released the breath I was holding, gripping on tight to my handbag as though it was a life raft.

"Merde," he said, "why don't you look where you're going, you idiot!"

A nervous giggle escaped my lips, then I spied the famous glass pyramid of the museum and sighed, uttering a prayer to the higher power who had performed a miracle by getting us this far.

When Jean-Paul swung into an underground carpark and pulled up the handbrake, I was out of the car like a whippet, grabbing my makeup case and was across the concourse in seconds. "Merci," I called to Jean-Paul over my shoulder and headed for the nearest doors.

"Hey, you know where you're going?" he asked.

I swung around and considered his question. Then looked up at the signs and frowned. "No," I admitted, "I don't speak French."

He nodded, a slight quirk to his lips. "You crazy English. You'd better follow me." He sauntered off in the opposite direction, chuckling to himself.

A few tourists had taken an interest in our exchange and looked on with amusement as I lowered my flaming face and trotted after him.

As we exited onto the street, we traipsed towards the

Seine, following a steady stream of tourists.

"Is it far?" I asked, juggling my makeup case.

"No, not far. I like the walk. It's good, 'eeps you 'ealthy," he said, patting his chest.

"Oh, but the smoking?" It slipped out before I could stop myself.

"I'm trying tu stop. My wife, she nags."

My mouth dropped open. Crikey, he'd nearly smoked a packet waiting for me. I couldn't imagine how many he went through when he wasn't trying to stop. When we veered to the right, leaving most of the tourists behind, I wondered whether I should have asked for proof of who this man was?

"Are we going the right way?" I asked, gnawing at my lip as it appeared the entrance to the Lourve was behind us. I glanced at the street name; Rue Rivoli. Not that it would do me any good if I needed to do a runner.

"De Louvre 'as quatre entrances. We'll use the Passage de Richelieu. Come, it is just up 'ere."

By this time, there was just a splattering of people walking the streets. Then Jean-Paul led me towards a somewhat ordinary entrance, in a rather tatty cream building with what appeared to have graffiti on it, a shiver shot up my spine.

"Are you sure this is the place?" I asked, putting one foot on a flight of concrete steps that could lead anywhere, and the least likely place would be Paris' world-famous museum.

"'Urry, they will lock the gate any minute." He gave a

salute to a guard, and they spoke briefly in French as if they were old friends.

I looked at the iron bars about to be closed. "Is this the traitor's gate?" I asked with a humourless chuckle.

Jean lifted an eyebrow. "You think you deserve to be locked up?" he asked.

I snorted and followed him up. "Only if you read the British tabloids."

He flicked me a puzzled look and then guided me through a maze of corridors. Finally, we entered the main museum and then crossed another corridor, entered a doorway that led to a large airy room with a buzz of actively going on. A woman in a chic black sheath dress, with multicoloured bangles with a scarf at her neck and red pumps, came to greet me. If it wasn't for the accent and bracelets, I would have said this was Eve's French counterpart.

"Beth darling, 'ow nice to meet you. My name is Lily, and I am the head makeup artist. I 'ope 'ou had a comfortable flight, and Jean-Paul 'as made you welcome? Jean is our creative director. It was..." She looked at him and when she saw he had engaged in conversation with another staff member, said, "Lucky 'ou arrived in one piece, 'e is a terrible driver." She smiled and led me over to the most beautiful woman I have ever set my eyes on, sat at a dressing table surrounded with lights. I avoided my reflection in the mirror and smiled at her warmly.

Reaching out my hand, I waited for her to shake it. After a moment or two of hesitation, I realised, she would not reciprocate the gesture, I brushed my hand awkwardly down my body and said, "Hello Demais, my name is

Beth and I'm here to do you makeup this week. Is there anything I should know before we start?" Trying not to gawp at her flawless cocoa skin, luminous chocolate eyes and perfect features.

"Thought she was the expert?" she said to Lily in a strong London accent.

"She is dear, but Beth has only just flown in from London.

"Didn't she prepare on the flight? Ain't that what you're supposed to do when you 'ave the pleasure of working with an international super model and risin' film star?"

"Hello, I am here," I cut in. "You can discuss any concerns with me directly. I only knew I was coming to Paris, half hour before I left. So, if you'd just like to tell me whether you are allergic to anything, we can begin."

"You know I don't talk to staff," she said to Lily. "And I don't care for excuses. Very unprofessional. Lil, give her the notes, I'm really too fussed to be bothered with all this." She closed her eyes and pouted like a petulant child.

My face burned, and I tried to control my shaking hands. Lily laid a calming hand on my arm. "It's been a very long day for Demais. I'm sorry if she came across rude."

"I heard that. An' I ain't rude…"

Demais continued her rant, still with her eyes closed as Lily led me away and whispered into my ear, "Please don't mind Demais, she is an enfant gâté, nothing more. But we 'ave to pamper such children. "Ere are the notes. For today, if you can give her a light, fresh faced look with a splash of colour. We will take photographs this evening among the sculptures in the Richelieu wing."

I nodded my head, took hold of the notes, and studied

them. And to think I gave up the date of the century to come here tonight. I needed my bumps felt.

Continue the story in :

PLAIN JANE - Book 2 - Sexy Beast

Out Soon

Available to Pre-order June 1st 2022

info@rebeccarayneauthor.com

https://rebeccarayneauthor.co.uk

Other titles by Rebecca Rayne:

Cherry Sweet - Submission is Strength - A BDSM romance

Soft Domme, Victoria Clayton meeting country boy Sam Myles, an innocent to the world of BDSM, should she lead him down this path? Sharing a connection the pair are drawn to each other. Is this the start of a beautiful love story?

And please, please take the time to leave a Review.

Thank you.

REBECCA RAYNE

ABOUT THE AUTHOR

Rebecca Rayne

Rebecca Rayne lives in Essex with her husband and two teenage sons. All her life she's been an avid reader and over the years has made several attempts at writing books, but never felt she had the necessary skills to do them justice. Then, like many others, in lockdown, she started helping her youngest son write a 500 word creative writing piece. 19,000 words later she realised this would turn into a book.

After writing three more, she joined writing groups and realised where she had a lot to learn.

Her debut novel Cherry Sweet was released on Amazon in 2021.

Romance has always been a passion. Veering away from Erotic fiction, temporarily, she sat down to write the Plain Jane series.

Plain Jane - Beastly Pursuits is book one in the series.

She plans to release 3 more, but being a fly by the seat of your pants type of gal, she knows she'll likely be tempted to write another erotic book.

If you like variety, with a strong romantic connection, you'll love this author.

Contact Rebecca on -

rebeccarayneauthor.co.uk
info@rebeccarayneauthor.co.uk

Follow on -
Twitter https://www.twitter.com/rebeccarayne
Facebook https://m.facebook.com/214374320603715
Instagram   https://www.instragram.com/
rebeccarayne_writer/

Printed in Great Britain
by Amazon